Be Brave Always

♥ Kris

Stain
By Kris Jordan

Published by Brave Girls Press™
Golden, CO

Jordan, Kris, Author
Stain

Cover design Design Dog Studio
Interior Design: Andrea Costantine
Editor: Donna Mazzitelli

ISBN 978-1492264286

1. Young Adult
2. Fiction
3. Mental Illness

STAIN

Kris Jordan

Dedicated to my mom, Robbi,
September 15, 1952 - August 30, 2012.

Acknowledgments

I WANT TO thank my daughters, who inspire me to be more and better every day. I acknowledge the people in my life who have encouraged me and believed in me even when I couldn't. They saw things in me before I did, and for that I am forever grateful. In naming one, I would need to name them all, so I will simply leave it with a thank you. You know who you are. And finally, to God, who created me and continues to guide and love me…always.

Prologue

THERE'S AN AMOUNT of denial required to make a relationship work. There are some things we have to overlook to keep the peace. Some people may call it being naïve—but then everyone is naïve, or self-protective, or both. I created the world I needed at the time. It's like a softer version of multiple personality disorder. After all, isn't every psychological condition just a stronger, more obvious, more extreme case of something "ordinary" people do? As if any person is ordinary…

My delusions, I now see, were my best friends—the Ones that looked out for my happiness. Truth made me unhappy. My delusions were not quite a betrayal, because they were the tools that kept me safe—until now. I guess that's why the journey hurts. Uncovering truth hurts. But so does the dilemma that fights itself out in this journey called life—the battle between fantasy and reality. At least that's how it was for me.

You might think that my discovery started when my mom attempted suicide, or when I saw my dad again, but I think it began the day Debbie and I got in the car and bravely left in search of something unknown. Hoping for something better.

Chapter One

WHEN I BRUSH my hair back, it flips up on the end, like the perfect cheerleader's ponytail. But I don't wear a ribbon; I just pull it back, as tight as I can, until it yanks at the skin on my face. I'm not a cheerleader either. I'm just a regular girl. Well, maybe not as regular as others. I like music, all kinds. I think that makes me different. I listen to any combination—from opera to classical to metal to punk. My art is kinda that way too…classical and punk. Flat, smooth strokes and bumpy, gloppy oil blobs. I love the idea of opposites on the same canvas. Really, the dynamics of opposites—that they may not be opposites all the time. Maybe they fall on a circle, next to each other in one sense, then back to opposites in another. Like love and hate.

My body is like that too. I'm short and skinny. Perpetually a little girl frame with an experienced old soul. Someone told me that once. Even my blue eyes make a unique combination with my boring straight brown hair. So, I pull it back, away from my face, and let my eyes shine. Teachers always ask me if I wear contacts, but I don't. I add a tiny bit of blue eyeliner to bring more attention to them and leave it at that.

I take after my mother, physically anyway, and maybe even artistically. I like to paint, and she likes making crafts, especially silly ones like painted rocks with googly eyes, or mosaics made from any kind of hard material, or mash-ups of photos with heads switched onto mismatched bodies. Well, when she's healthy.

She's very different when she's not. She puts on weight with her medication, and then she loses it all again in her "down," when she doesn't eat.

Like her, I look younger than I am; Martha, my mom, says I'll appreciate that when I'm older. People always think she's a lot younger than she is. She appreciates it for sure; her boyfriend Leonard is twelve years younger than her. Leonard's not mine or Debbie's dad, though. Mom had me when she was twenty and Debbie when she was eighteen. That's when she was still married to my dad, right after high school. I'm seventeen now, and I can't imagine having a kid when I am eighteen, or ever really. I don't want kids.

I remember when we (Mom, Debbie, and me) first moved to Cleveland; we moved into an apartment. I hated that I couldn't run like I'd been able to do when we lived in the red house in Colorado. There, I didn't have to worry about the noise I was making or disturbing the people downstairs.

In our house in Colorado, it was quiet. Sounds were made by us or by a person driving up the driveway. There were no surprising sounds there, not even the time when Mom slammed the door and ran out of the house screaming that she was going to leave. She jumped into the car and took off for a few days, and we weren't surprised. My sister and I just kept digging at the dry soil, patting it into mud pies with cups of water, topping them with bright yellow dandelions and trimming our masterpieces with pine needles.

In our apartment, the many sounds of cars passing by, neighbor noises, and washing machines off kilter jolted us, putting us on edge. It was awhile before everything became mundane and regular and we, or at least I, settled in.

I was thankful when we moved into another house. I was in 5th grade by then. My sister Debbie and I nicknamed it 66. Nothing creative about that, it was just the house number. And, the house looks just like houses 2 through 65 on the left and the right, and on every other road that make up our neighborhood. Debbie and I joke that no one is good enough to be number one, because the area was developed as low cost housing to allow more people into suburbia. Numbers 65 and 66 are Mrs. Flanagan and us, and our houses sit at the curve of the cul-de-sac that makes up Cambric Court.

On Saturdays, I usually work a long shift at the skating rink, but today I'm home. I hear Mom in the kitchen, slamming dishes into the cupboards and cussing. The smell of her cigarettes makes its way to my bedroom. I tuck my journal into the bottom of my pants drawer. When she is angry, she gets suspicious. It is best to hide the journal while I have a chance, rather than wait for my bedroom door to fly open. I keep it disguised: a blue spiral-bound notebook clearly marked with the word "homework" across it in large black letters.

The notebook represents the true me, including every inch of my vulnerability; Mom seeing it would bring inevitable death. But I did remove one page completely, just in case. It was too risky to keep. I still remember what was written on it. Just the torn edge in my journal reminds me, even more than the written words ever would, of what I once disclosed. My greatest fear is my mom discovering my true feelings about her, about Leonard, and mostly about myself. I tore that page out and burned it, that scary page with my real heart spilled onto it. Even so, I still keep my journal, like Holy Scripture, buried in the walls of a house—hidden, bound, and sacred.

Martha learned about something called "red flags" from her therapist. I think the therapist was trying to get Mom to look at her own red flags, but instead Mom took it as permission to remove all of our privacy. She kept nothing sacred; she even barged into the bathroom without apology, her accusing look disappearing within seconds as she "caught" me wiping my butt.

Placing locks on doors was out of the question, and even the doors themselves became problems. "Our only doors will be those that leave the house," my mom said as she proudly removed the bathroom door with the Phillips' screwdriver, the scabs on her knuckles revealing the destruction from the previous week. Everything was to remain open to avoid suspicion and allow for help, "in the name of trust," she said. It is just the opposite, though; trust keeps doors in proper order, not stacked in the garage with their hinges hanging loosely like broken teeth dangling from a mouth.

She later returned the doors, after Debbie, in her belligerence, stood in the bedroom doorframe boldly observing Martha and Leonard doing it. Of course, even when the doors were returned, a hole remained where the doorknobs had been.

Walking down the hall, I see Mom in her long, baggy nightgown. It's a dirty old t-shirt of Leonard's and hangs to the middle of her thighs, exposing her bony knees. Her frantic pacing, her twitchy movement, tell me she's furious about something, or nothing, as usual. I watch her childishly stomp around the kitchen, a cigarette trembling in her hand. Mumbling, she bites her nails between puffs and vulgarities. She's disgusting.

"Bastard! Leonard! Late again, cheatin' bastard!"

She pauses long enough to scream my name. She doesn't notice me standing behind her.

"Rachel! Ra…" She turns and her glassy eyes catch mine, "Put these dishes away."

She moves her hand toward her ear. She's trying to hide the cigarette burns, but I've seen them.

I grab the hand towel and start on the pile. She pours herself a cup of coffee. Stale, I'm sure—made last night in the early hours when she couldn't sleep. The carpet muffles the thuds as she stomps down the stairs into the basement.

Leonard spent last summer finishing the basement, including the installation of a full bathroom. He did it in the hopes that if Debbie had her own space, she might pay a little rent; maybe feel more grown up, or show some responsibility, or quit whining, or something. But Debbie is a tornado. And I'm the one who cleans up after her, and Mom. If I'm not literally picking up Debbie's junk, I'm lying to Mom about where she is or gluing back together the knickknacks Debbie's thrown into the wall during a tantrum.

Debbie hates Leonard and all attempts he makes for conversation or friendship or fatherly-figure advice—anything, really. She told me that she thinks he's a fake. That he must have something wrong with him to hang out with a woman like Mom. A woman a lot older than he is. A woman with children. She thinks he's creepy and needy.

One time, she came out of the bathroom screaming at him, "Put the seat down. This is a house of women!"

She told me he needed to get his own place, not just because of the stupid toilet seat incident, but because she found a couple nudie magazines in the garage.

"This is OUR house," she told me. "No one asked if we wanted him here. He's just another of Mom's mistakes."

Whatever.

Debbie no longer lives with us. She moved out a little over a year ago, awhile after Leonard moved in. I think Debbie just wanted an excuse, any excuse, to get out of the house, to prove she's an adult. Something she's failed at time and again. She is too dumb to realize that if she just quit using drugs, she'd be halfway there.

✳ ✳ ✳

Confident Mom is completely settled downstairs, I creep quietly toward her bedroom, avoiding the creak in the hall three steps dead center outside her door. In her private bathroom, cluttered as always, is a drawer filled with her medication. I check it every so often to see if she's still taking them. I count her pills. I know when she gets her refills because I pick them up for her. Her weight loss made me start checking again. And now the cigarette burns tell me she's slipping, but her pills are right. Double checking, I pour the pills into my hand and count them back into the bottle two at a time. The amount is correct. Maybe the burns were something else. I close the bottle, the drawer, and the bedroom door and go back to the kitchen.

Leonard walks through the door as I take my first step onto the linoleum. "Where's your mom?"

"Downstairs. Can we talk a minute?"

"Tonight, okay?" He winks at me and smiles his great smile and heads down the stairs.

Leonard is the peace in the house. He understands me and listens and knows how to calm things down.

"Leonard!" I hear Mom bellow.

"Rachel, call 911!" Leonard yells up to me.

"Why, what happened?" I shout back as I run down the stairs, "Mom!"

I see her supporting herself against the wall, arm extended, covered in blood. The wild rage I feared my whole life is now here, in her eyes—senseless, deranged, delirious. Her arms look like they'd been caught in a tiger's mouth or a lawn mower. There is so much blood. All over her. Her neck, her arms, her shirt.

"Go away!" she pants at me. "You've done enough! Look what you've done to me! Look!"

She snatches my shirt, yanking me up against her bony body, so close her coffee-cigarette breath invades my nose and repulses me. Every part of her repulses me, and I feel nothing but disgust for her. Her breath is hot and her saliva is gurgling in her throat like angry growls.

"*Sssee*? What *choove* done?" She slurs.

I can see her sliced arms now, cut from her wrists to her elbows and side to side around her forearms. Her throat too is ripped with thin slashes. "No," I spit, "You did this." I push her away as I step back.

She hits the wall and looks at me defiantly, the same look I've seen in Debbie's eyes. She throws herself against the wall, smacking her head hard enough to knock herself to the ground. She reaches out to pull herself back up, scratching the plastered walls, tearing her fingers against its texture. Then, she collapses. Her blood drains from her body into the carpet.

I hear Leonard hang up the phone, and it interrupts the flood of everything that's happening in my brain.

"The ambulance is on its way." I hear his voice like an echo in my head.

I once watched a man spin cotton candy onto a paper cone at a carnival, half in anticipated pleasure of its sweet taste and half in disgust over its dry, chalky texture. I watched him spin it around and around. That's how my mind feels. I don't know if Leonard understands this. He looks at me with fear in his eyes. Maybe he's afraid she'll die, but I think he might be even more afraid of the look in my eyes. Maybe it's a wild, manic look of accusation and guilt, as if I've killed her. Maybe even a look of pleasure. I don't know what my eyes are saying to him. I don't know what my heart is saying to me as it twitches erratically in my chest. I step toward him for an embrace, but he runs up the stairs.

My mind hums as I snatch a towel off the back of the couch and drop to the floor. I attempt to rub the blood from the carpet, but instead, it just spreads, becoming one big stain.

I rub harder, reach farther. My sweat drips into my eyes, burning them. I smack Mom's foot, forgetting she's there. Fury builds in me. I want to pound on her, to let it all out.

A hand grabs my outstretched arm and a strong hairy arm, Leonard's arm, wraps itself around my waist and lifts me to my feet. He drags me to his car and drops me into the passenger seat. The sky is bright, like an exploding star; it snaps me into the moment.

"Are we leaving? I need a bag."

Leonard looks at me with a confused look on his face, "No, Rachel, no."

The wind blasts my skin. My head responds to the sudden movement of the car, but I tighten my neck. My molars grind into each other. My jaw aches.

"Do you understand what that was about?" he asks, sounding defeated. I don't know what he means. *Do I understand why she did this? Do I understand what will happen now? Do I understand why I am in his truck driving away? No.* Yet, lethargically I nod yes because I know that's what he wants to hear. He wants to know everything will be okay.

"You understand then. Right? You get why this happened, don't you?"

I understand there is no rhyme or reason when it comes to Mom. That's all.

I look at him—at his sad eyes. I know this look. He tells me he doesn't know what to do, that he has to leave. I feel my insides dissolve as though my soul knows something my mind won't accept. I think I understand, but am I supposed to really? *Am I supposed to understand why he is leaving?*

We stop and he helps me out of the car. He knocks on the twelve of the stenciled 112 on the door in front of us. I'm on Debbie's doorstep. Leonard walks away before the door is answered. I hear his truck door slam and know that he's gone. He got in his truck and drove away. I didn't need to hear the engine fire or the clutch pop. He ran away. Just like Debbie. Just like everyone. They all run away.

Chapter Two

I STAND ON Debbie's straw doormat and contemplate running, but my feet and brain feel paralyzed. A pencil of a man answers the door. His dirty brown hair is pulled back into a low ponytail and his shirt is off, revealing pale skin stretched over his skeleton. He eyes me with a lustful look, as though I am a gift for him. His eyes drop and his grin fades as he notices the bloody smudges on my shirt and knees.

"Rach?" My sister's voice asks from behind him. He turns to expose us to each other.

I take two steps into the apartment, and the man guides me to the side so he can shut the door behind me. Debbie is engulfed in a sunken yellow couch and doesn't look surprised to see me.

"Hey," she says, motioning for me to take a seat

next to her. "Leonard called and told me what was going on. You okay?"

I don't answer. Mildly dazed, I look around. Two girls lounge on the floor beside a muscular blonde who's holding a game controller in his hand. The girls are boring in appearance, and despite the heat, they wear black, long-sleeved shirts. One is lying on her stomach, twirling her feet around in the air as she flips through a *Rolling Stone* magazine. The other is sitting cross-legged beside the blonde, her talon of bright green acrylics staking claim on his knee.

Cigarette smoke swirls, then vanishes in the sunbeam glimmering through the sliding glass door, above the TV and their heads. Outside beyond the tiny concrete slab patio is a steel fence and a single tree. A blue jay hops onto one of the branches, causing the branch to bounce. I want to lie down and sleep under that tree, in the coolness of its shade.

"What the…?" The blonde, groaning from his virtual demise, turns from his video game's explosive death to gawk at me.

"Chuck, not now," Debbie responds. She stands and guides me to a bedroom at the back of the apartment. The heavy eyes in the living room fail to provide the warmth I need. Who cares what they think anyway.

Debbie pushes the bedroom door open and grabs my wrist to drag me in. *Am I a toddler?* I yank it back. Without the slightest hint of distress, she snatches a towel off a hanger in the closet and marches into the bathroom. She looks back at me, "Are you coming?"

I reluctantly follow and plop down on the edge of the bathtub. Debbie locks the door and hands me a brush and rubber band and wets one end of the towel. She drops in front of me and begins washing my knees and legs. Perplexed, I watch her. She appears nurturing—maternal even. I haven't seen that since we were children. Once, she helped me mend my scrapes, after my failed attempt at learning to ride a bike. The pavement had been smooth, but even after she lowered the seat on her bike it was still too big for me. I fell hard. She had apologized and cleaned me up, just like now.

I can't hold back a sigh or the tear that escapes down my cheek. Debbie crawls in closer, wraps her arms around my waist, and rests her head against my stomach. I slide to the floor and sniffle back all I want to say to her. I hold her and imagine pouring out all my pain. I wipe the line of tears off my cheek and notice dried blood hiding in my cuticles and on the fine hairs of my fingers. I stand to wash them and catch my reflection in the mirror. Debbie sits quietly on the floor watching me.

I feel yellow, like how being drunk looks—clammy skin, smudged eyeliner. I take the towel and wipe my forehead and cheeks. The heat brings red blotches to my ghostly looking face. Debbie finally speaks up, "Rach."

I hear her but don't respond. She never asks questions. She always looks at me as though we have some secret bond, some silent communication. There's none. There were so many times I needed her to listen and she wouldn't. She'd just shoo me away, like my emotions were petty compared to hers. What did she know?

"I'm tired," I say flatly.

"You can lay down in the bedroom. Stay here as long as you want."

Standing and touching my hair, she watches me, trying to read my face instead of saying what I want to hear. Something like, "Rachel, I'm a terrible person for leaving you behind," or, "Will you forgive me for being such a selfish, self-absorbed bitch all these years?" She says nothing.

"No. I don't want to stay here." I begin brushing my hair to move her hand. I can't concentrate. I want to be alone. I want silence. "Can you just take me back home?"

"Yeah," she answers, resigned, "But I don't have my car until after ten. I let Juliessa take it to work tonight."

Crap. I'd have to stay. "Can I borrow a shirt?"

We go into her bedroom, and she takes out a shirt from a dresser that seems ready for the junkyard, then we head outside to sit under the tree.

I dream of blackness brightening to red, the color of the sun through my eyelids. The color of my mom's blood on the rug. That stain forever an image on my brain. Debbie's voice wakes me.

"Come inside. Come on, wake up and come inside."

I sit up and pull my knees into my chest. "I'm okay here for now." I feel a momentary breeze of serenity.

"You wanna talk about it? You want to tell me what happened?"

Her question sucker punches the peace off my face. It wasn't a nightmare; everything that just happened was true. The sleep didn't reverse it.

"I'm sorry I wasn't there."

How can she be sorry? She left us. Her hand trembles slightly as she lifts the lighter to the cigarette hanging between her ashen lips. She inhales and blows the smoke out and away from me, then continues, "I mean for everything. And I'm sorry I left."

My stomach drops, my throat tightens. *How can she say this right now?* I feel like vomiting. My emotions rise up and I feel the burn of bile in my throat. I choke it back down and try not to shiver as my sour-tasting feelings retreat back to my stomach. I am so pathetic, so weak. But I can't trust her. Not yet.

"Have you ever tried to find Dad?" I ask her. Debbie's face sinks. She looks at me blankly for a minute, then down as she takes another drag from her cigarette.

"Yeah. About two years ago."

"Did you find him?"

"Yes."

"Will you take me to him?" I ask, wanting to smoke her cigarette. I watch her inhale, contemplate, exhale. It is her yoga.

"No. He doesn't want to see us." She rises up and

walks inside, smashing the remains of her tobacco into the grass.

I wish I had my notebook. I'd write: "7/14: Debbie apologized." I wouldn't say a thing about Mom or Leonard or anything else. I'd divulge all that the next day. For today, Debbie apologized.

I head back inside the apartment and join Debbie on the couch.

"Bobby," Debbie begins the introduction to the pencil-man, "this is my sister Rachel." He begins chatting away and is friendlier than I expect. This is his apartment. He tells me he met my sister through some friends and he got her the job at the restaurant where they work. I look at Debbie and raise an eyebrow playfully, like she'd kept a secret from me. *She has a job? A steady job?*

"I'm doing good Rachel. I'm doing really good." She smiles at me. I believe her. I really do. I can tell she really wants my approval. I glance around the apartment and realize how ordinary it looks. There's a black and white Ansel Adams poster on the wall, a wooden table with matching chairs in the kitchen. I pick up a deck of cards from the table in front of us. Debbie scoots to the floor and then around to the opposite side of the coffee table.

"Deal me in," Bobby instructs, "House rules?"

"Rummy," Debbie says before I can, picking up the cards I already dealt and shaking her head. She remembers our game. Bobby acts surprised but retrieves his cards anyway.

The three of us are laughing wildly when a tan-skinned young woman unlocks the door and comes in. A smile crosses her face, and I am instantly jealous of her beauty. Her smooth chestnut hair hangs in a sturdy braid down her back.

"Juliessa! This is my sister," Debbie says, trying to hold back her laughter.

"You started the party without me?" She pulls off the blue vest with her nametag attached and throws it over the back of a chair. She walks into the kitchen and emerges with shot glasses and a bottle of some kind of alcohol. She sets one in front of each of us.

"Are you in?" Juliessa asks before pouring.

I shrug. She shrugs back and pours the clear liquid into all four glasses.

"A toast!" Juliessa pronounces, raising her small glass. Debbie and Bobby follow suit. I hold mine up with theirs, mimicking their ritual. Juliessa's eyes glisten, "My brother's out of jail tomorrow. Your sister's come to visit…"

She grabs Debbie's shoulder like she is congratulating a co-worker on a promotion, "A shot for family!"

Juliessa, Debbie, and Bobby throw their drinks to the back of their throats, and I imitate them as best I can. The burn hits my stomach before my glass hits the coffee table. Debbie and I stare at each other for a minute. I've never had a drink before, and I think Debbie knows it. I wait for our silent communication to kick in.

The warmth of the liquor settles in my stomach, and the alcohol begins to sedate my fears.

"Whoo-hoo!" Juliessa shouts and I laugh at her dramatic reaction. *People do that in movies, not real life. Do they?* She pours everyone another shot and Bobby deals another round of cards.

I spread my cards and look out the corner of my eye at Juliessa. Her high cheek bones and smooth, cappuccino skin make me wonder if she is Hispanic. I wish I was Hispanic. No, I wish I had heritage. Something to identify with—something bigger than me. Something I can be proud of.

I push down as far as I can the heritage of mental illness. If I crush it way down deep, into the smallest part of me, maybe it will vanish. If I keep it bound tight enough, maybe it will never reappear.

Awhile back, I read a *National Geographic* about how other cultures bind their feet or stack rings around their necks. The researchers were amazed at how quickly people could alter their bodies, like accelerated evolution. In the end they realized it wasn't evolution at all, just people distorting their own bodies. The tribal Africans didn't stretch their necks; they lowered their shoulders, actually deforming themselves. What the Africans considered beautiful doesn't really exist—they thought they had beauty, but the reality was they'd become disfigured.

Mental illness is already a deformity for my family. If I accept it, I will succumb. It will win me like it won my mother. But if I control it, if I twist, wrap, bind, and restrict it, mental illness won't be able to overcome me.

I drink my next shot, my mind holding onto progressive golden rings until a fanatical heat runs toward my brain like molten lava. I cringe, then look at my cards. It takes everything in me to withhold a smirk. I can catch them all if the next card is right. I feel awake yet sleeping at the same time. Debbie discards the seven of clubs. A perfect card for my hand. I pick it up nonchalantly, slide it into place among my straight, and chuck the entire hand down. "Rummy!"

I spring up and raise my hands into the air and giggle at how free I feel in my lunacy. I fall back onto the couch and the threesome laugh at me.

"She's toast," Juliessa proclaims and pours more shots, leaving my glass empty. I don't care. Really. Bobby slides his hand up Debbie's leg and I smack it playfully.

"Stop it!" I demand, halfway serious, feeling a new sense of guardianship for Debbie.

"I'm fine Rachel." Debbie moves Bobby's hand onto her bare knee. She shoots me one of her layoff looks. In our fun, I had almost forgotten who Debbie really is. I am under the influence, not only of the stupid alcohol, but her lies. *I am an idiot. She tricked me. We have a terrible thing in common now. I've joined the ranks of the intoxicated! What was I thinking?*

I push myself off the couch and dart into the bathroom, almost falling against the sink. I reach to shut the door behind me, but Debbie is there.

"Are you okay?" There is obligatory concern in her voice. I want to cry. I grab a wad of toilet paper to wipe my nose. *I am so stupid! What the hell am I doing? I have more self-control than this!* I feel betrayed by my own body. And I am angry at Debbie for doing this to me, breaking down my guard and letting me be so… flippant. I wish I could fight Debbie and all the lies around her. I can't though. Because I'm a stupid little wimp. I'm afraid of feeling and of the damage I will do. So, I scream. It's a ridiculous obnoxious scream, like a toddler's. "Debbie, you haven't changed! Nothing's changed!"

My voice is high and shrill and panicked. There is no way I can stay here. She makes me out of control. I hate her. I hate me. "I'm going to find Dad."

I don't know why I just said that, or where it even came from. Debbie looks at me with a stunned expression. I try to hide my own surprise with a "so what do you think of that" type of look. Her irritation is beginning to show. I grasp the counter to brace myself against the empty spinning pain behind my eyes.

"You are so stubborn! What is *wrong* with you?" Debbie shouts, cursing something and storming out of the bathroom. I splash water on my face and take deep breaths. I look in the mirror at my pink cheeks, then head back to the living room.

Debbie is smoking a cigarette; a memo pad rests in her lap. When she sees me she hurls it at me.

"That's Dad's number. Maybe he'll want to talk to *you*." She takes a long drag from her cigarette. "Maybe the Goddess Rachel…" She trails off under her breath and reminds me of our mother. "Bobby, throw me that pack."

He tosses a box of Newport's to Debbie.

"Will you take me home?" I ask, knowing it's a futile question.

"I'll take you," Bobby offers, receiving a glaring look from Debbie.

"Not until morning," she instructs. He looks at her with his eyebrows pushed down into the ridge of his bony nose. "Sleep it off, Bobby." She glares at him, then staggers to the bedroom.

✳ ✳ ✳

The couch is comfortable, or maybe my numbed body doesn't notice or care that it's not.

Bobby is sitting at the kitchen table when I wake up. He stands slowly and winks at me as I gradually sit up. He grabs his keys and wallet and motions toward the door with his head.

Surprisingly, we get into Debbie's car, apparently the shared vehicle. Bobby sits down, almost smacking his head on the door as he enters. He pushes the seat back, cursing at Juliessa's shortness, immediately lighting a cigarette and turning up the music. "Major cross street?" he commands.

I shout my response, thankful it's too loud in the car for us to have a conversation.

I begin pointing directions after we get somewhere I recognize. "Turn there at the cul-de-sac," I shout over the music.

He turns slowly. At night, I would be able to know if anyone is home because of the lights. Today, I have no clues. The manicured bushes against the house are like statues, revealing nothing. My guess is no one's inside. Yesterday, the driveway was no doubt crowded with police cruisers and an ambulance. Today, it's stagnant and quiet as cement. I know they kept Mom, but I don't know for how long. I wonder where Leonard is and if he'll be here tonight.

"Doesn't look like anyone's there?" Bobby says more like a question than a statement.

"Yeah, well." I hop out before he offers any more wise observations.

More than likely the front door is locked, so I decide to try the back. If it is locked too, there is a key under the troll next to it.

I open the side gate and walk through. The pointy-hat, ceramic troll sits still as stone with a brainless smile on its face. He used to scare me. His expression is creepy, the kind that makes you wonder if his eyes watch you or if one day he'll sneak in your room. I jump at Bobby's voice. "Everything okay back here?"

Why hadn't he left? I put my hand near my throat, pretending to not be scared. "Fine. Yes, I'm fine."

I lift the key to the lock.

"I thought maybe you'd invite me in." That look is on his face again. That slight smirk, that tilted eye, a look of persuasive flirting. I'm not interested.

"You should go. Thanks for the ride, and tell my sister I'll call her from Dad's."

Bobby takes a step toward me, and all of a sudden I feel like a gazelle. My ears perk and twist, my hair stands on end, and I find myself fighting the intense desire to run. I step back.

"Rachel? Is that you?" The elderly voice of our neighbor Mrs. Flanagan, Mrs. F as I call her, rings like a church bell over the grassy plains.

"Yes, Mrs. F," my voice sounds exhausted, "It's me."

She comes around the fence in her flowered robe and ankle-high booties. I am, for the first time ever, grateful she is a nosy busybody.

"Oh, hello, young man," she says, extending her frail hand to Bobby. "Get on your way now." She smiles as though she'd said, "Have some oatmeal cookies and milk." She pulls her arm, now hand-and-hand with Bobby's, toward the gate.

"Um, I'll let your sister know you'll call her." Bobby looks like a child being dragged by his ear as he walks back to his car. I can't help but chuckle to myself. *What a jerk!*

"Sweetie, are you okay?"

"I'm fine. Thanks." I turn the key in the lock.

"Is your mom okay? When will she be back?"

"I don't know, Mrs. F." I say, pushing the door open.

"Are you here all alone, then? You can come stay with me." She smiles and I smile too. Why doesn't she understand I'm not the same little girl in footsy pj's curled up on her couch? That was when I needed her. I don't anymore.

"No thank you." I shut the door with both my hands and turn the latch.

Chapter Three

THE KITCHEN LOOKS just the way I left it, dishes stacked on the towel exactly how I placed them yesterday. The only difference is a business card on the table with a gold-embossed crest on it. The card belongs to Patricia Ayote, our social worker. She is responsible for, in her words, "setting up positive adult resources" for me. In my words, "finding ways to invade my privacy."

She isn't completely horrible, though; she did make arrangements to place me with Mrs. F instead of a foster home during one of Mom's lengthier hospital stays. Patricia is moving quicker now; twenty-four hours haven't even past yet and she is already harassing me with her arrogant card. Granted, Mom's hospital trips, with one exception, have not been as dramatic as this one. Patricia probably has our phone tapped and gets notified immediately if an ambulance is called—everyone knew it was just a matter of time.

I walk to my room without turning on a single light. My legs feel heavy; my arms long, like the tips of my fingers will brush the ground at any second. I pull the paper out of my pocket with the number Debbie gave me. I dial, certain it's a fake. I sigh at the chimes and voice informing me that the number is no longer in service. It doesn't matter anyway. I never intended to go and see Dad; if anyone had answered, I would have hung up.

I slowly place the receiver back down. He never came for us. For all I know, he has another family, happy and healthy, somewhere in Colorado. I plop down at my computer and type into the search field: Donald White.

There are about fourteen pages of responses. Not a surprise. No less than the last time I looked. *What was I thinking? It's not as though his face will come on the screen with a plea to meet his missing daughters.*

I reach behind me to my backpack. I've been waiting for this reunion. My journal! It's safe for me to have it out now. It's safe for me to be me. When something is always with you, it's like it *is* you. And when you are apart, you feel lost, even though nothing is lost…just apart. I wonder if Dad feels lost too, or if it's just me.

I check the side pocket for my cell phone. Sometimes I wonder why I bother paying for it. I really don't have anyone to talk to anyway. I check it for a voicemail, but there's nothing. I dial Leonard and only get his voicemail, so I don't leave a message. He will see he missed my call.

Our conversation on the way to Debbie's repeats in my head. *What did he mean exactly?* I want to talk to him. I have questions. I call him again and leave a message this time, telling him just that.

Maybe he will be home tonight. Maybe we can talk then.

The blue light of the computer screen stings my eyes as I sit biting my lip. The words come into focus, the bold repeating words mocking me. *Did you mean "Donald White"? Find "Donald White" on Amazon. Donald White, Facebook.com.*

I close the screen and start another game of computer solitaire.

✳ ✳ ✳

I hear the phone ringing.

"I'll get it," I call to Mom, pulling my hands out of soapy dishwater. I pick it up, but it still rings…two, no, three times. I open my eyes and jerk up, still in my bed. No dishes, no Mom, only a ringing phone. I jump out of bed, but the caller has hung up or it's gone to voicemail.

After a quick bathroom visit, I check the message. The familiar, elderly voice of my neighbor breaks the silence of the house.

"Rachel? Sweetie, I found out what room your mother is in. Let's see, it's one now. I'm leaving in about an hour if you want to ride with me. I'll stop by before I go."

I've slept for two hours and feel refreshed enough to go and see Mom. Plus, I'm pretty sure Leonard will be there, and I need to see him. I crank up the radio, strip and jump into the shower to get ready.

✳ ✳ ✳

Mrs. F knocks on the door and I giggle to myself. The door usually isn't locked, and her knock-proceed entrance is hindered today. She shakes the knob violently and calls for me.

"I'm coming." I shout as I swing my backpack over my shoulder. The house doesn't feel as cool, quiet, or vacant as when I first arrived. It feels like my home again. I meet Mrs. F at the door and lock it behind me.

Mrs. F's car smells like leather and peppermint. I tuck my backpack between my ankles, but should have put it under me. The seat's just burned layers of skin off my thighs, I'm sure. "Ow!"

I press my feet into the floor and keep myself lifted for what seems like an hour while Mrs. F adjusts the crocheted seat cushion, then the mirrors and her seat. *Isn't she the only one who drives this beast? Why is she adjusting everything? Does it readjust when she exits the car?* I'm suffocating and feel my skin crisping from the 1,000-degree seat. The first blast of air conditioning is like a blow dryer. I wipe the sweat off my nose and from under my eyes with the back of my hand as she finally pulls the car onto the road.

The hospital is only about five miles away, and I've made the trip many times before. I haven't seen the newest renovation, though. Judy, the greeter there, said she hoped they would add more parking.

I still get butterflies every time I approach the hospital. The pure natural greens, reds, and lavenders of the landscaping glimmer in contrast to the sterile, stark whiteness of everything inside. Actually, the hospital normally looks regal with the sun glowing behind it, but today the building just looks like a huge obstruction. Even the full, leafy trees—meant to offer solace and hope—seem gloomy now, or maybe it's just my mood. It's depressing knowing people are sick and dying here. And Mom is one of them. I do want to talk to Leonard and clear up what he was talking about, but even that seems gloomy. I wonder why I've even come.

There isn't any extra parking, and after circling several times, Mrs. F finally does a ten-point turn into a spot beside a Suburban at the outer edge of the lot. I push the vanity mirror down, comb through my hair with my fingers, and apply some lip gloss. I open the door and instantly wish I hadn't. The moist heat chokes me. Mrs. F steps out of the car, fights to get her keys into her purse, and almost steps into moving traffic.

"Mrs. F!" I cringe, but the car stops just before hitting her. She looks at me with a smirk, like life is a game. Mrs. F shrugs, then waves at the driver, who slowly proceeds past us. I smile, reminded of how silly she can be sometimes, and walk closer than usual to her as we enter the hospital.

"Room 418," Mrs. F tells me and I point to the elevators. I notice the new tile in the foyer, but the alcove between the elevators is the same. A four-foot tall bronze statue of Jesus patiently lingers with all who wait for an elevator. His elbows are tucked in; his forearms stick out, with palms raised. A burdensome robe hangs over him, his head and eyes staring out at the floor. There is discord in those eyes and the offer of humble guidance in his outstretched arms. The elevator bell rings, breaking my gaze and summoning me to the fourth floor.

A food tray sits in front of the nurses' desk—reminding me I forgot to eat today and am now hungry. The nurse looks up at me and then Mrs. F speaks, "We are visitors to Martha White in room 418."

"Sign in here please," the nurse says, then looks back down at the chart she's studying. She looks over at our names, smiles awkwardly, and points toward the left with the pencil she's holding.

Mrs. F nods at her and we head down the hall. By the time we are outside of the room, I can barely breathe.

"Mrs. F, I'm gonna get a drink. I'll be right back." I take off before she can say anything. When I turn around, she's already vanished into the room. I bite my lip and fingernail at the same time as I walk the narrow hospital corridor.

I don't want to see her—her body swollen with fluids or starved like death. I don't want to hear her voice. Weak and fragile or manipulative and condemning. I

don't want to see her face, with her wiry lips and accusing, pathetic eyes. I don't want any of it.

I press the down button for the elevator, suppress-
ing the urge to run as far as I can. *Honestly, though,
where the hell would I go? There's no one and nowhere waiting for me. There's no place in the world for
a sixteen-year-old to start over.* The elevator rings as I
hit the lobby where I can take a sharp right toward the
cafeteria for some lunch. The doors slide open and as
recognition of that down-turned head, pointy nose,
and long blonde hair hits my brain, Patricia Ayote
smiles. If there is any skillful way to hide, I don't pos-
sess it.

"Hi, Rachel. I was just coming to see you." She
looks at me slyly with her crystal-blue eyes. She is a
Barbie, a down-to-earth Barbie if there is one. She's
wearing olive-colored slacks with a matching jacket
that hangs open to expose a ruffled white blouse.
Both end fashionably at her waist in a still-looking-for-
Mr.-Right, thirty-something sort of way.

She sports a thin black belt, matching heels, and
carries a briefcase in her hand. She could be mistaken
for a professor, lawyer, or pharmaceutical sales rep,
if she wore her hair back. She is tough and usually
fair, but hard to manipulate. I've tried. Right now she's
standing in front of me with a look on her face that
says, "I know you won't return my calls, so I will pursue
you like a kid looking for her favorite candy in a Halloween sack."

"Hi Patty." I fake smile and scoot past her as
though she doesn't have the authority to ruin my life

with two small but mighty words: foster care. The heels on her practical, yet stylish, shoes click as they hit the floor behind me.

"Can I buy you lunch…or have you already eaten?" She asks. Her questions are always loaded, so I tell her what she wants to hear.

"Yep. I made myself a sandwich at home earlier," my stomach hears my lie and grumbles in response. "I'm just getting some coffee." I'm annoyed with myself. I could have a free lunch if I would just drop the attitude.

"Great, we can talk while you're enjoying it."

We walk quietly into the cafeteria, and I eye the a la carte spread, individually proportioned dishes aggressively suffocated in plastic wrap. I am so hungry, everything looks good. I pour and prepare my coffee as slowly as possible, sipping it as I meander to the cashier. Patty stays by my side, more patient than I'd ever be, with a smile on her face that must be painted there.

"So," she begins as we sit beside a glass wall that faces out to the hospital's landscaping. "What's your plan?"

"What plan? Do I need a plan?" I stick my finger into my coffee to stir it more.

"Your mom is going into Bethesda House after this. You know that. We can do a temporary placement for you again, or you can go to Elements."

She folds her hands together and sets them down on the table in front of us. I look out the window. Elements is a halfway house where they send misfits. I'm not like those kids—cutters and petty thieves whose parents let them run wild.

"Well, you know I'm not going to Elements. I'll stay with Mrs. F."

"Rachel, we both know that can't happen again. Last time you were with Mrs. Flanagan, you took advantage of her kindness and ended up in trouble. As far as I'm concerned, you lost the privilege to stay with her again."

I turn to look at her. "I told you before *I wasn't drinking*. I was with the wrong people at the wrong time."

She leans forward toward me, but low, like she has a secret to tell. Her hair stops short of falling into my coffee. "Honey, if you hang with the wrong people, you eventually will get stuck with them at the wrong time and in the wrong place."

She sits back and drops her hands into her lap.

"Well, I'm not going to some halfway house."

"Okay, well then," she reaches into her bag and pulls out a worn manila folder. "I have a family that will take you," she pauses, looking at some scribbling to confirm, "The Rochesters."

She jots something in an empty area of the folder and circles it. She is left-handed. I never noticed that before. She sets the pencil down like it is decided.

"Sorry, Patty, but I'll go live with my dad before I go into foster care." I lean forward and am louder than I expect to be. I feel like my final playing card is down.

I take another sip of coffee, wondering if she will call my bluff. Unfortunately, she doesn't look surprised and my inner smirk drops.

"That'd be great if we knew where he was." She stands. *I'm losing her, losing my chance to get my way.*

"Wait! Debbie knows where to find him."

"You talked to Debbie?" She pushes her chair in but is still holding on to it.

"Yes. And she says she knows where Dad is, so I can go and stay with him." My heart is racing, but I try to show calmness. Patty's eyes move, like she is thinking hard, trying to remember something. "Technically, if Debbie is sober, you can stay with her, since she's eighteen. If she has a safe, drug-free home and is willing—"

I roll my eyes and cut her off. "No. She doesn't qualify."

Patty sighs, "Okay, well then, I will get your mom's approval on the placement and contact your father. You need to have his information to me tomorrow so we can get this thing going. It could be a few weeks, and if Mrs. Flanagan won't take you in the interim, you will go into temporary care, agreed?"

Sucks, sucks, sucks. The whole plan sucks. At least she's conceded to let me stay with Mrs. F...for now. "Okay." I lie for the fourth time in less than an hour, including acting like I still have coffee in my cup. She walks away, and as soon as she's out of sight, I jump up and throw my cup in the garbage can.

Threatening to find my dad has been coming up a bunch in the past few days. A part of me does want to know him, to meet him and have a relationship with him. My excuses for not caring, or not wanting to see him, are fading. I want family.

With Debbie gone, I only have Mom and Leonard. But now with Mom in the hospital and Leonard missing, it seems as though I need a new family. I thought Leonard would be here for me. I thought we were family. *Where did he go and why isn't he calling me back?* Part of me is scared. Scared Leonard has run away. Scared to find Dad. Scared Dad won't like me, scared I'm not good enough, scared he never wanted me in the first place.

Just as I approach, the elevators open to reveal Mrs. F standing there.

"Here you are!" She motions for me to come into the elevator. "I just talked with Ms. Ayote and she asked me if I would watch out for you this week."

I watch the numbers light up, seeing Mrs. F out of the corner of my eye. Her smile and her heart are so big; I wonder how I could have ever hurt her. I am so lame. I turn to her and smile back.

"Now, let's go see your mom. Ms. Ayote is talking to her right now." My smile drops.

"Mrs. F? I'm not really in the mood to visit her. I mean, it's just too much, you know?" I must look really sad because she hugs me, and this time I let her. It is one of those pressed-against-saggy-breasts-and-starched-ruffles types of hugs, the kind I've dreaded my whole life, but it feels really good right now.

"Yes. Yes, dear. Let's go." The doors open on the fourth floor and the nurse looks up just as they close again. We descend back to the lobby and out the door—back to her house—my house at least for the next week.

It is quite refreshing leaving the hospital. The sun warms my body, slowly defrosting me after the arctic temperature in the hospital.

"Mrs. F?" I ask, sounding as innocent as possible, "When we get home, I have a couple things to take care of…to get ready…so I can stay with you." I stumble over my words as I think of what I need to do. *How to not hurt her and not stay.*

"Oh, of course. I happened to grab extra turkey at the store today, so we'll have that for dinner, and…"

She's rattling on about groceries and asking questions without getting my answers, planning out the week's menu with the inventory list of food items she has on hand at home. My cell phone rings, interrupting her monologue. I snatch it, hoping it is Leonard, but it is Debbie's number. I ignore it.

I nearly jump out of the car when we pull into the driveway. Before slamming the car door and running away, I lean back in to where Mrs. F sits perfectly straight-backed behind the steering wheel. "I'll be in back in a few minutes."

"Okay…and after dinner," she calls after me, "it's *Mary Poppins*!"

✳ ✳ ✳

"Donald White, please."

All my calls start the same. This time I barely wait for a response.

"Speaking." The voice on the other line sounds too young, but I try anyway.

"Hi, my name is Rachel White, and I am looking for my father."

I cross his name off as soon as this Donald says, "I'm seventeen."

The gamut of responses, everything from, "You're kidding" to "How old are you?" to "Don't call here again," are impossible to sort out. How am I supposed to know if the angry, accusing, slammed-down phone is really him? How am I supposed to know if the man who says he'll meet me is my dad and not a pervert? What if Dad *is* an angry pervert? I throw my notebook with the list of Donald Whites across the room.

It is time for dinner, so I turn off the lights and head over to Mrs. F's house.

"Oh, glad you're here. I was just coming to get you."

I crack a weak smile and sit at her round kitchen table that's covered with a sky blue tablecloth and a clear plastic protector. She sets a plate on the table in front of me. It's covered with a thick turkey sandwich, ridged potato chips, and a scoop of macaroni salad. Her plate is missing the chips. She sits down and sighs.

"Rachel, Ms. Ayote—"

"Patty," I interrupt.

"Patty called and told me your mom won't agree to send you to your father's." The bit of turkey sandwich sticks to the roof of my mouth.

"I'll get a court-appointed guardian! Mom's not thinking straight. She can't make that decision," I retort.

"Sweetie," she sets down her fork, "You can't go. Your mom has a certified letter stating that your father is denied custodial rights and you are never to see him. She refuses to list his name on any paperwork." Her eyes begin to water as she reaches for my hand. "I'm sorry."

I bite my sandwich and chew it slowly. I am too hungry to abandon it, but every bite feels like it's fighting me to go down. I take a drink of milk and feel it coat my stomach.

"You stay with me this week," she puts a spoonful of macaroni salad into her mouth, places her napkin over her lips, and pats at her nose—trying to hold back tears.

I am going to have to run away. I knew that, but I will think about that tomorrow. Tonight, I will watch *Mary Poppins* next to Mrs. F, and I'll make my plan in the morning.

I fall asleep on the couch sometime after Jane and Michael jump into the chalk drawing. I wake up to a peacefully silent house. I wonder why I can't wake up every morning like this, feeling the warmth of the sun fill the room and the smell of fresh herbs in the air from Mrs. F's cooking.

I sit up, drop my feet to the floor, and question if I even want to move. *Can't I lay here forever? Do I really need to even take one step today? Couldn't I completely ignore my life for just one more day?* I lie back down and close my eyes. My phone rings, startling me. I see that it is Leonard and answer as quickly as I can.

"Leonard! I've been trying to reach you! Where are you?" I am overwhelmed with emotions. All of a sudden, I'm shaking and feel my throat tighten.

"Rachel…"

"Leonard, I'm going into foster care at the end of the week!" I am hysterical, excited, and frightened, longing for him to come and rescue me—finally.

"I know. I got your messages. Listen, you can't call me anymore."

"What?" I'm so confused. "I need your help. You're the only one who can help. I need you to get me out of here." I am frantic, desperate. *Why is he doing this*?

"I can't. I can't do that."

"What? Why not? I need you. Please…please Leonard." The silence hurts. I feel my nose begin to run.

"Rachel, I told you in the car. Don't you get it? Do you have any clue what's going on?"

"Apparently not! What do you mean? Let's just go. Let's just move up our plans and go away together now." I fight back tears. I feel exhausted, like I am teetering on the verge of a cliff, unable to grab hold of it.

"Your mom knows you like me. She knows. We… you and me…we are responsible for this. I should have never let you believe I liked you. I should have set you straight. I'm stupid and I'm sorry. I could have gotten into a lot of trouble…if it had gone any further…you don't know how close I was…I can't…I'm a jackass and I'm sorry." His voice breaks up, and not because of the connection. "I messed up, bad…" he sniffles, "…and I am sorry. I can't help you. I don't love you. We aren't going anywhere together. Please, please… don't call again."

The phone goes silent. He hangs up and might as well have shot me in the head. I stare at my phone, then run to my house. Whether absolute panic, or rage, whatever it is that's coursing through me, it doesn't matter. It feels good. I throw open drawers—kitchen drawers, dresser drawers, cabinet drawers. I throw them down like garbage, spilling their stupid secrets all over the floors. Mom's medications, useless as they are. Bills, clothes, silverware, measuring cups, none of it means anything.

"What?" I scream to the ceiling, to the stars past it. "What is he talking about? We made dreams together! We dreamt of a life away from here! He told me he would kiss me my first kiss at sunset the first day we left! That we would make a life together and it would make me so happy! No more dealing with Mom. We wouldn't have to worry about what she was going to do next. What's happening? What does he mean?"

I pound my fists. I push anything and everything that's in my way. I want to destroy everything inside me—everything outside me. Everything!

I collapse onto the floor and have a tantrum—

a true toddler one with arms and legs flailing and pounding the ground. In all its glory, and because I can, I shout as loud as possible at all that my life is.

Rage and crying feel good. Really good. I lay on the floor, exhausted from feeling and yelling, yet strangely refreshed, like how a volcano must feel after purging the lava from its core. My plan develops as I lay there, swimming in the buzz of adrenaline. I will put together a bag with snacks, a pillow and blanket, and I will pull out all of my savings. I will take the bus to Colorado and look for Dad. I'll have better luck there, locally, than on the Internet. I am going to find my dad. I am scared, but I can do this. I will leave in the morning.

Chapter Four

WILL I FIND HIM? Will he even want me? I've been through this stupid argument a million times. And every time, I make up an excuse to not actually do this, but now I don't have a choice. Do I? I won't go into foster care! I shove another set of clothes into my suitcase.

I call Mrs. F and apologize for running out of her house. She says she understands that this is a difficult time for me. She tells me she had checked in on me and wonders if I slept on the kitchen floor all night. I assure her I didn't and delicately ask her for a favor. After a long pause, she agrees to take me to the bank and bus terminal.

Inside the bank, I withdraw the four hundred twenty-eight dollars I have in my account. I stash some of it in a pocket of my purse but keep out two hundred to put away in front of Mrs. F when I get back into the car. She acts like she doesn't see me, but I know how nosy she is. I thought if she saw the money for herself, maybe I wouldn't have to endure her questions. I'm wrong.

"Is that all you have sweetie?"

"Yeah, but it's okay. I'll have enough." She slides her liver-spotted hand over to me and presses a crumbled, indistinguishable amount of money into my hand. She brushes her soft lips against my cheek and kisses me gently. I close my eyes, feeling the hum of love in my ribs. She is the closest thing to a grandmother I have ever had.

"Do you have snacks?" she asks.

I nod.

"Coins for the payphone?"

"I have a cell phone." I wonder why she doesn't hand me a checklist. I'm sure she created one moments after I heard the drawer slide open this morning when I called. I opened that same drawer once, smelling the mint of the multiple packs of gum she keeps there. It also holds Post-it notes and sharpened pencils for times that require checklists. Like now.

Mrs. F. loves Post-it notes. They litter her mirrors and fridge door. Old grocery lists, new grocery lists, phone numbers, reminders. They clutter her space the way thoughts make my mind feel at times. Like now.

"I don't want to miss my bus."

I say it airy and light, hating that I push her away. I don't push too hard, though. Despite my annoyance, her cookies and starched shirts are always a constant, and I have few constants. She knew me when I was a child, but she doesn't really know me now. She doesn't understand that I grew out of the snack-and-story-time she once offered. She doesn't know how to answer me when I ask where my dad is or why my mom can't get better or why people hurt other people. She can't answer me anymore.

As I look at the bus station, though, I realize I don't really want to be brave and adventurous. Why can't I slip on those footsy jammies and curl up on Mrs. F's couch? I wait for her to offer that so I can stay with her again. The silence is uncomfortable.

"Thank you," I pause and swallow. "Mrs. F, I know you could get in trouble for this, you don't have to—"

"I'm an old woman. I forget things all the time." She smiles at me slyly. I sigh, thank her again, and step out of the car.

The bus station looks foreign. It isn't as romantic as I expect it to be—the way it's portrayed in movies. I hope Leonard shows up. But that only happens in movies too. The second message I left him might cause him to turn up, restoring things to the way they were before all this. *Why do things happen that way?* Things can be fine and well one second and then, in the blink of an eye, nothing is recognizable.

I hold my head up and walk deliberately to the ticket counter. I don't have anyone to mimic except what I have seen in movies—so that's what I do. I hate looking like I don't know what I'm doing, like a fool. I like to be prepared, planned, in control.

My phone rings and I reach into my pocket, praying it's Leonard. Instead, it's Debbie. I push the button to ignore it. Within seconds, it rings again. Again, Debbie. She is being persistent today. As I answer, I feel a hand on my shoulder.

"Love your ringtone," Debbie says as I turn around. She was calling me so she could find me in the crowd. She reeks of smoke.

"Don't you know that smoking causes cancer?"

"It will be my cancer, not yours," she replies. "I want to go with you."

She scratches the back of her neck and looks down to the floor.

"Why? How did you find me?"

She doesn't answer. Instead, she asks me if I already bought my ticket. I shake my head no.

"Let's go together. I'll drive. We'll pack camping gear so we can stop along the way."

"Debbie, I don't understand."

"You can't go out there alone, and we're family." And then, as though she read my mind, she says, "I went to Mrs. F's to talk to you. I got there just as the two of you were pulling out of the driveway. I followed you and Mrs. F here. It actually was perfect timing. I might have missed you, but I didn't. You drove right by me and didn't notice that I was there."

I'm speechless as I look at her, trying to examine her face and the thoughts behind it. Of course, I don't want to go alone. *But can I trust Debbie?*

She got me drunk at her house, so I know now

what it's like to be high and stupid like she gets. She left me to deal with Mom in all her crazy. And she was the one who stole Mom's pills to get high and sell the rest for money. She didn't care about anyone but herself. And she always lied about it. She would look Mom right in the face and tell her she'd gotten home on time, that she hadn't broken the frame on the family photo, or that she was going to class when she wasn't.

Debbie tucks her arm in mine, like a friend, not like a mother, and waits for my response. I wait to see if she will pull my arm, force me her way, but she doesn't.

"Okay," I say, "We'll go together."

✳ ✳ ✳

This is the first time Debbie and I have been in our house together in over a year. It is still ransacked from the night before, the evidence of my fit of rage. I'm embarrassed that it reflects my inability to maintain my sanity. I ignore it and am glad Debbie does too. I think we are both good at ignoring craziness.

I pull down the attic ladder and climb up. I've been up there only once, many years earlier. Mom told me not to go up there because the flooring is so weak I might break it and fall through. She uses it for storage, mostly stuff we cleared out of the basement. I remember when we labeled boxes and Leonard hoisted them up.

The attic is hot and dark. I reach around for the string attached to a bare light bulb. Wiry insulation brushes up against me and makes me itch. I take another step up the ladder and finally find the cord. I yank it and the attic comes to life. It's bigger than I remember. Thin boards are laid across the planks where boxes and supplies rest. Why these planks don't cover the entire attic instead of just a corner, I don't know. It's like an Indiana Jones movie, where the treasure sits comfortably on its perch yet the obstacle you have to get around is dangerous and unstable.

I slowly climb up and posture myself on a four-by-four crossbeam. The boxes, labeled in my handwriting, sit in neat rows: Blankets, Baby clothes, Camping, Christmas, Files, Halloween, MISC. I scoot carefully toward the camping supplies. Beside the box are the sleeping bags, rolled up tight. I grab one and throw it through the opening in the floor. It disappears to the hallway below. I throw down the second. Debbie tells me she is bringing them into the living room. We work in silence as I hand her supplies. I don't know what some things are, or if they have anything to do with camping, but I pass them down anyway. We will go through them safely on the floor instead of fumbling through them while I balance precariously on wooden beams.

One last box marked "camping" looks too big to simply throw down. I open the box and look in, but I can't see anything distinguishable. I shift and rock it, moving it slowly so I don't accidentally send it through the ceiling. I look through the opening in the floor, "Debbie!"

Getting no response, I continue to shift the box toward the ladder. I will have to get below it to heave it down further. I stand up carefully, ducking my head so I don't bump it on the roof, and place my feet on the wooden plank, like I'm on a balance beam. I giggle as I almost tip over, grabbing the beam above my head for support.

As I balance awkwardly, a black-and-yellow shoebox in the corner catches my eye. I tiptoe my way to it and discover it is taped shut with duct tape, too strong to break with my nails. Curiosity gets the best of me, so I head down the ladder to open it below. That way Debbie can help me with the big box later.

I puncture the tape and tear it open. Inside are clippings from newspapers, a yearbook, and some other mementos from Mom's teenage years. There's a picture of her undefeated JV softball team, her name appearing in bold letters as the team captain. I open her yearbook. She and Dad met in high school. I flip to find his picture, nervous to see if I resemble him or even know his face. Donald White isn't listed. I turn to look at pictures of the other classes. He isn't there either. *Didn't they go to the same high school? I thought they did.* I check the senior pictures again, and Mom's face jumps out at me—Martha White. *Wait.* I look back at her softball picture. *Martha White.*

Her maiden name is White? Mom never changed her name? I have been looking for Donald White, but that isn't my dad's name. The weight of this thought feels like I'm being buried alive, the dry desert dirt pressing against my coffin, keeping air from reaching me as I slowly die. Could it really be as simple as us having the wrong name? *The wrong name?*

I frantically sift through the box, searching for a picture or a name for my father. Nothing is clicking. I rush back into the attic and look for more unlabeled boxes. No luck. I grab the box marked, "FILES," and frantically head back down the ladder.

"Debbie!" I shout again for my sister, more shrill than I intend. She runs around the corner, a worried look on her face, "What? What's wrong?"

"Dad's name! It isn't Donald White! White is Mom's maiden name. Were Dad and her married?"

We sit in silence for a moment, questioning our memories, testing our thoughts against what we believed was true.

"Our last name was always White. I wrote it that way in elementary school. I remember." Debbie spoke slowly as she thought back, trying to jog her memory and mine.

"Yeah," I agree. "In school, I never wrote anything but Rachel White."

We look at each other as though our faces will trigger Dad's last name. I grab the file box and we search for birth records, marriage license, tax forms, anything that might have our father's name on it, but find nothing. It's as though he never existed. *How will we find a ghost?*

Chapter Five

DEBBIE AND I look at each other—perplexed, tired, defeated.

"What should we do?" I ask.

"I think we should just go."

"How on earth will we find him? We don't have his name. We don't know if he even lives in Colorado. What if he never did?"

Debbie stands and goes for her cigarettes. Pulling one out of the pack, she responds, "Rachel, what else can we do? I mean, do we just hide out and wait for Mom to get out of the hospital and do this all over again? Do you go into foster care?"

I think for a moment, "So we just hit the road?"

"Well, what were you gonna do when you got off the bus? Just bump into him? How are we any worse off now than we were before? If we go and look up the wrong person, we'll be there instead of here—that's the only difference. I think this could be a clean slate for us."

Debbie is right. I don't have any more or less of a clue now than I did yesterday about who my dad is or how to find him. I guess I expected things would work out. I had hope. But today, I don't have even that. If we don't find him quick, we will run out of money and end up stranded in Colorado where we know no one. I guess at least I will be with Debbie and not in a foster home. More than anything in life, I am terrified to live in a stranger's home, without my things, without my own space and rules.

"Okay. Let's get a clean slate." I feel sick even saying it.

"Let's start with a trip to the grocery store." Debbie smiles.

✳ ✳ ✳

I am used to buying groceries. It is one of the chores I enjoy. Mom isn't a good shopper. She seems to buy all junk food when she is in an "up" mood and food doesn't even cross her mind when she isn't. I enjoy the grocery store like it's a school field trip. Leonard and I would do the shopping, the whole time talking and laughing and planning meals.

I grab some apples, paper goods, and protein bars, trying to block further thoughts of Leonard from my mind. I look over at Debbie, who is going for chips, Twizzlers, and Gummy Bears.

"Yum. Roasted Gummy Bears. Those should work just fine on a campfire." I mumble sarcastically.

Debbie rolls her eyes. After I'm satisfied we have what we need and are within my budgeted sixty dollars, I push the cart to the checkout lane. Debbie throws a map into the cart. It's the most responsible thing she's done all year.

Debbie jumps on and rides the grocery cart as it zooms across the lot, bound for the car. The wind blows through her hair and she giggles. "I'm really excited about this Rachel!"

I envy how carefree and energetic she can be sometimes. Mom is like that too at times—like nothing on earth bothers her. For me, my mind doesn't seem to ever get quiet. Except with music. Or cleaning.

We load up the snacks in the backseat and dump some ice and Cokes into the small cooler.

✳ ✳ ✳

I wake up in the backseat with my backpack under my head. The sun is just coming up; Debbie has driven since we left at midnight. I sit up slowly, then crawl to the front. My stomach is grumbling and complaining that I haven't eaten. I pull an apple out of the cooler. "You want anything while I have this open?"

"Nope," Debbie responds.

"Okay." I eat the apple more heartily than I expect. Debbie is grinding her teeth and tapping her hands on the steering wheel to an unheard beat. I've seen her do this before—this staring off without direction. Probably deep in thought. Maybe she is thinking about Mom. A thought sneaks into my mind that she might be high.

The radio scans to pick up a signal, stopping on a country station. She punches the scan button again. Another country music station.

"There are a few CD's in the glove box." I hear her try to fumble for it. I pop it open and push through the collection, grabbing a brightly colored case. A profile of a woman sporting big hair, outlined by several neon lines, graces the paper insert. "25 Greatest Hits of the Eighties! Performed by the Actual Artists! As seen on TV!"

I push the CD into the player, then stare out the window. As farms pass by, I wonder if people think about what it's like to live in the city like I wonder what I missed by growing up there. The farms, upright and sturdy, conjure images of hayrides and festivals and love stories. The flatlands are freckled with blobs of color. As we approach, the colors become cows, houses, mailboxes, and trees. Appropriately enough, Mr. American Countryside himself, John Cougar Melloncamp, sings to us from the radio. It is the last track, and the quietness when he's done singing brings me back into the car.

"Aren't you tired?" I ask Debbie.

"No, I'm good," she responds. "I just keep singing this song in my head and it keeps me going." A sly smirk crosses her lips, "Maybe you know it."

She pauses to look at me with an invitation of challenge in her eyes, and I know exactly what she is thinking. In unison, loud enough to wake farmers in the nearby fields, "I'm Hen-er-ay the Eighth I am! Hen-er-ay the Eighth I am I am!"

We get louder and louder, trying to be louder than each other, then end in booming laughter. It is a song we used to sing with Mom when she was in her "up" mood—dancing around the house, picking up plants to dance with and make us laugh. She would blare rock n' roll and pretend to hula, and we would laugh. It was such a great memory, such a carefree time, that this song became our inside joke against Mom whenever she started ranting.

"Oh my god!" I laugh, "I nearly peed my pants!" I bend forward, trying to hold my bladder, "No, *seriously!* Can you pull over?"

Debbie, laughing and pounding her palms on the steering wheel, slowly eases to the side of the road. "There's a roll of t.p. back there," she says, pointing to the backseat. "Go ahead and go. There's no one out here."

I look around, and sure enough, there is no sign of anyone. I grab the toilet paper from the backseat and climb out, still giggling. The air is crisp and dewy, like the apple I ate. Six a.m. is the prettiest hour of the day. Mist settles on glass; the sun threatens to come up, its warmth confined to the glow of its brilliant colors. I take another deep breath and cough as cigarette smoke fills my lungs. Debbie is outside the car, inhaling the cancerous smog by choice.

I leave the doors open to make my own little stall,

just in case someone comes by, and position a squat. I watch Debbie, who takes the opportunity to stretch. Still smiling, she takes a deep breath of air and turns toward me. The field behind me catches her eye. It's a beautiful plowed field of corn stretching back as far as anyone can see. She dashes for it and a fence meets her at chest level.

"Rachel! Can you smell that?" She calls to me.

"What? Cow dung?" I joke.

Debbie laughs, "No! Fresh country air!"

"If that's what you want to call it!"

I watch Debbie climb carefully over the wire fence and run into the field. Full, weedy grasses brush her legs. Her feet sink into the wet dirt trail around the crop. Reaching straight in front of her, she grabs a husk, sniffs it, and yells, "This may sound stupid to you, but I never realized these were so tall!"

She looks up to the top of the stalk. "Corn actually grows! And not all chopped up and canned or frozen and bagged like what Mom always gets. Fresh. Clean. New!"

She sounds like a woman liberated, throwing her arms out and tipping her head back as though she is a corn stalk herself. I laugh again, zipping my pants. "Get out of that field before someone shoots you!"

Debbie runs back to the car and spins around. "There was a kid at school who said that he used to visit his uncle, or some other relative, on a farm. He said that the kids would tip over cows for fun! Tip over cows!"

Debbie looks at me, her eyes wide like a young child with a new box of crayons. She spins around again, then falls into the car seat. "Okay, we're off."

And with that, our heads shoot back as Debbie spins the tires, shooting dirt at the magnificent cornfield.

❋ ❋ ❋

"So, did you tell Bobby you were leaving?"

"No."

"You don't care about Bobby?"

Debbie fakes a laugh, "Maybe once I cared about him, but that was when I thought he cared about me."

"He let you stay there rent-free after everyone else threw you out. To me that sounds like he cared about you."

"He didn't *let* me stay because he was nice, Rach," Debbie says, shaking her head.

"What do you mean?"

There is a long silence. She doesn't answer me. I cross my arms. *Is she really going to play the silent game this early in our trip?* "I'm only two years younger than you, Debbie, and sometimes you treat me like a baby. You have no idea what it's been like for me."

"Listen, sleeping with him was my way of paying the rent, okay? He didn't care about me. He had no reason to, I guess. He got what he wanted out of the relationship."

"I don't believe you." *Who would do such a thing?*

"Me staying there meant that he got laid on call. He won't miss me."

My face is hot. I don't know if I'm shocked to hear my own sister talk like that or what. "You could have come home," I mumble, turning my head toward the window.

"Rachel, no matter how I lived it was better than living with that bitch and her asshole boyfriend."

"He's not an asshole. Leonard saved Mom." I bite my lip. I shouldn't have said that.

"He did, huh? Then what's with this last *episode*?"

I don't want to answer her. I stare out the window. She continues as I knew she would, relentlessly.

"You know, I hope she doesn't recover this time. I hope this is it. No more."

"Debbie! Stop it. Stop talking like that." I put my hands over my ears and squeeze my eyes closed. "I'm not going to listen to it!" But despite my attempts, it doesn't block out Debbie, who becomes louder in response to my defiance. She goes on about how horrible our mom is. She calls her names and screams the stories I've heard time and again: "Like when she got thrown out of the JC Penny for shouting at the clerk… arrested for stealing that necklace…passed out in her car…exploded the microwave…"

"Stop!" I barely say the word. She continues, "And candy-ass Leonard always there to save the day, making excuses, believing her lies…"

Bright bursts of light begin to explode behind my eyes. "STOP IT!" I scream. Debbie falls silent. Typically, these headaches only come on with stress or dehydration. *What if this is the end for Mom? Why is*

Debbie being so shitty? Why can't I have a normal life like other kids? Why did Leonard turn on me? What the hell am I doing in this car with Debbie?

Debbie pulls into a rest stop and lights a cigarette. I jump out and the cool air blows across my face like a gentle kiss. It is welcome until the nausea of my headache surges. I stretch to break the tension in my neck and back. I roll my head around and squeeze my shoulders, breathing in deeply. I've cried myself a headache. No more crying. No more headaches. I get back into the car and watch Debbie as she sticks a new box of cigarettes into her shirt pocket, looking at a large foldout map and walking back to the car. She plops into the seat, still looking at the map over the steering wheel.

"Only about an hour to St. Louis. We can go see that thing there…the arch. I got a pamphlet. That would be nice, wouldn't it?"

I nod, mostly to not continue any more conversation. I could care less about tourist attractions.

"I'm much more cheerful with coffee," Debbie announces. Her face becomes somber, "Rachel, I'm sorry for what I said…about Mom…she'll be okay. And we will too."

I close my eyes and tilt my head back. The car begins to move.

Chapter Six

"I'VE GOTTA PEE," Debbie grunts as we pull into another station. She walks away, catapulting a cigarette butt across the parking lot moments before she walks in, throwing the door open as she does. I rub my temples. Even after a full bottle of water, my headache remains.

I wonder if Debbie has any aspirin. If not, I'll go into the station. I open Debbie's duffel bag. My hand bumps something hard, so I pull it out to look at it. It's a frame small enough to only hold a 2x3 snapshot. The picture, cut down to fit, is of Debbie and me. I look about two or three years old. I don't remember ever seeing this photo before, and I can't tell where it was taken. The background is unfamiliar. I use my shirt to wipe the glass clean so I can look at it more closely. Then, I smile at the two of us and put the framed picture back in her bag, leaving it on top. I will ask her about it later. I reach in again and find a small canister. Thank goodness! Aspirin! I drop four into my hand and swallow them with a swig of Diet Coke.

Craving a sweet snack, I decide to head in. I should maybe take a bathroom break too.

As I cruise down the snack aisle looking for something interesting, I see Debbie exit the bathroom and head for coffee. She pours herself a cup without any cream or sugar—*yuck*—and walks to the counter.

"Rough night?" The pleasant young male clerk asks Debbie.

Pushing a twirl of hair behind her ear, she cocks her head and looks at him, "Just long. We're driving through from Cleveland."

"Home of the Browns."

Debbie looks at him strangely, "I'll be honest, I'm not—"

"I'm sorry. Sometimes I get chatty around pretty girls," he smiles. "You're not big on football?"

"Right." She responds, shooting him a flirtatious look.

"If you don't mind me asking, where are you headed?"

"Colorado." she sips some of her coffee.

"Really? Well I hope you take some time to see St. Louis."

"Yeah. We are gonna stop to see the arch." She is such a flirt and she loves it. I think the clerk is cute but not really her type; he looks like he does crossword puzzles and reads in his spare time. I plop my goods on the counter next to her coffee and smile gently, breaking up their little love fest. Debbie asks for a pack of cigarettes.

"Can I see your ID?" he asks with a wink. She pushes it across the counter to him. He reads it aloud, "Deborah Victoria White. Yup, you're eighteen. Brunette, blue eyes, very pretty ones, five foot six and… did you lie on that last part? I was told most women lie about their weight."

She snatches the license back, hiding a grin. "And what are your stats? Actually, let me guess." Debbie flirtatiously eyes the clerk. "Your name is Tim…"

His name tag clearly states this. He adds, "Timothy *Samuel* Jacobs," stressing the middle name.

Debbie continues, "Age twenty-one. Six feet tall."

Tim corrects, "Twenty and six foot one," then adds, "Single. Enjoys romantic walks through the candy aisle and dinner by fluorescent light."

Debbie laughs. I smile but am getting bored with the interaction.

"It was nice to meet you, Timothy," I interject, tapping my granola bar on his hand.

"Tim," he corrects.

"Tim, we need to go."

We smile and exit, but Debbie stops short and stands outside the gas station door to smoke and linger so Tim can oogle her more. He takes the bait and stands in the doorway talking to her. I decide to dig through Debbie's bag further. Nothing too great—

some concert ticket stubs, a gold chain, a pen, a bookmark with a tassel. Printed neatly on the shiny, yellow bookmark is: "Love is patient, love is kind. It does not envy, it does not boast, it is not proud. Love always protects, always trusts, always hopes, always endures."

Debbie finally heads my way so I zip the bag, leaving the bookmark out, and toss it into the backseat.

"He was cute in a nerdy sort of way. Do you think?" Debbie asks as she plops into the seat.

"I guess."

We leave the parking lot and take what feels like the same highway on-ramp that we took eight hours ago.

"Hey Rach, there's lots of fields around here. Do you think we'll see any cows? Should we try and tip a cow, like my friend told me about? I've never done it. I don't know if it hurts them. I don't know if I could even get close enough to one without freaking out. What do you think?"

I hear her, but don't really feel like I am in the car. And I don't feel good. Like my brain is drowning. "Deb? I don't feel good."

"What? Ya gonna puke?" Debbie looks at me with a silly grin, waiting for the punch line. Her expression drops and she pulls over with a large swooping yank. "What's wrong?"

I open the car door and fall out onto my knees. Debbie grabs me, saying something about her bag.

I shake my head, "Aspirin..."

"Aspirin…black canister?"

"Umm." I moan, feeling my eyes roll back.

"Shit no. No! How many…Rach…how many did you take?"

My brain turns off and everything goes black.

I heave forward, then open my eyes. Debbie is cradling me, her fingers in my throat, forcing me to gag.

I lurch forward again, heaving. This time, the contents of my stomach spill onto the gravel.

"I'm sorry," Debbie is saying, repeating it like a mantra as she helps me into the backseat. We take off fast enough to rock me onto my side. Within minutes, I feel the emergency break jerk and Debbie jump out of the car.

Silence.

I feel moisture on my head and open one eye to see Tim holding a wet towel on my forehead.

I jolt as I feel myself being moved to a cot, no, a gurney. *Am I going into an ambulance?* I listen to the paramedics' commands.

Are they taking Mom again? What's happening? Why am I inside the ambulance instead of watching it drive away?

Past the ends of my toes, Debbie and Tim stand, shrinking as the distance between us grows.

✳ ✳ ✳

In my restful sleep, I feel wetness on my forehead that drips along my left temple and into my ear. I hear Debbie's voice, "I'm so sorry Rachel."

I'm lying in silence, unsure what's going on. I'm in a hospital bed. My stomach hurts. My throat hurts. The taste of charcoal coats my tongue. My ribs hurt.

I hear footsteps come into my room. They sound heavy, like someone's wearing boots. I slowly open my eyes and they roll back a bit. I hear a man's voice asking how I am. He is not a nurse. He's at the foot of my bed. He looks familiar. He is the clerk from the gas station. Tim. *What is he doing here?* I don't feel like answering.

He sits down next to Debbie and is silent for what feels like somewhere between five straight minutes and a half hour. My eyes pop back open when I hear her voice, then close again, as heavy as wet cement. I roll to my side to watch them. My eyes are almost completely closed, and I'm trying to understand what's going on. *Why do I feel like crap?*

"I'm sorry I was such a nut case earlier," she says to him, breaking the silence.

He ignores her comment and asks how she is doing.

She shrugs her shoulders and looks back down at the linoleum, "I'm okay."

I close my eyes again and the room has that same sterile coolness as when I've visited Mom. There's the same smells, same shadows, same sounds. I really don't want to be here. I open my eyes again. Debbie is leaning forward in her seat, propping her elbows on her knees. Her head is turned away from Tim toward the outside door.

"They just threw this at me and told me to fill it out." She lifts up a clipboard, then drops it back into her lap.

Tim picks it up and looks it over, "You didn't finish."

"Yeah, well, I don't know some of this shit."

"Is there someone you can call?"

"Not really, my mom's worthless, and we don't know our dad."

"How long has it been since you've seen him?"

"We were toddlers."

They sit again in silence.

"I don't know what to do." Debbie's voice reawakens me. "Rachel."

Debbie is over my bed. Her hand is on my shoulder.

"Rachel."

I open my eyes to see her face looking somewhat panicked. "Rachel, they want to call Mom. I gave them a fake number. I don't know what to do, but I think we need to leave. Can you walk?"

I am tired. She slides my pants up my legs. I manage to sit up and shimmy them over my hips. "Can I have some water?"

"Sure, of course." She pours me a cup of water from the salmon-colored pitcher into a sani-wrapped plastic cup, just like the ones they have in hotels. I find it funny and smile. The water feels good as it hits my parched lips, my dry tongue, and my sore throat. It is the best water I've ever had. Debbie is fumbling to put shoes on my feet.

"Rachel. We are going to go stay with Tim. You will be feeling better in no time. I don't want Mom to know where we are going. And I don't want us in trouble for being here in the hospital. I lied about pretty much everything, and I'm sure they're going to get suspicious really soon. Can we go? Are you okay?"

Of course I don't want to be here. She puts a hoodie around one of my arms. I frown.

"I'm sorry," Debbie says sliding the second sleeve onto my arm.

Debbie instructs me to stand and I do. She asks if I can walk. I am sure I can. *I didn't forget. Or did I?* My feet stay firmly planted on the ground.

"Walk!" I command them. They stay motionless. *Oh yes, I must bend my knees to get them to lift.*

"Bend!" I tell them and they do. My left foot raises from the ground and I throw it forward. It is a step. Finally, remembering what "walk" means, my right foot raises up and moves forward. I am walking. Just like that. I'm feeling a bit like a horse with heavy hooves, but I'm prancing forward just the same.

Debbie puts my hood up, and we plod out of my stinky white room. Debbie looks around like a spy.

I see Tim at the end of the hall in front of the elevator. He holds it open and waves his arm to encourage us. I'm at a full gait, moving toward the waiting elevator. Debbie pushes me into the corner by the buttons while she and Tim stand in the middle, like they are supposed to be there and I'm not. I'm hiding. The doors open, and Tim, Debbie, and I walk right through the sliding glass double doors of the hospital to our escape.

"I want water!" I demand. Tim opens the car door and helps me in. I lie down in the backseat. It's so much more comfortable than the hospital bed that smells like Mom's empty apologies, iodine, and the fruit Jell-O meant to cure all evils.

Debbie pulls out of the parking lot like we are leaving a bank robbery. I giggle a little, then fall asleep.

✳ ✳ ✳

I wake up to Tim's voice. I feel nauseous and tired and thirsty. I also need to go to the bathroom.

"See that next driveway on the left? That's mine," Tim is talking and points his arm out the car window.

Debbie nods. I can't see a house or a driveway. She slows down to prep the turn. A small light far from the street appears, and the headlights catch a dirt pathway leading to it. Debbie turns left, slowly rolling onto the gravel. I can hear tiny pebbles hitting against the undercarriage of the car.

"The driveway will fork left and there's a small path that heads straight back. Take that one," Tim says.

Debbie nods and follows the smaller path past the side of the house and stops just after one of the tires enters a dip in the road. The dust around the car settles. I wish I could see where we are, but it is pitch-black. Once the lights are turned off we might as well be in outer space.

"This is my grandma's house. I pay rent on the

back half. All we share is the kitchen, which is the best part of the house in my opinion."

Tim's smile and the opening of the car door illuminate the interior. He steps out but keeps the door open so we can see what we're doing. Debbie gets out and lights a cigarette. I scoot to the door and grab my backpack. My mouth feels dry again. I step out of the car and shut my door, then Tim's. I can't believe how dark it is. It takes only a moment for my eyes to adjust. The land becomes aglow from the moon. I look up to see the most amazing starlit sky. It looks like something from a romance movie—something I thought was made-up, like the Easter Bunny.

"It's beautiful," Debbie breathes. Tim takes her arm and guides her toward a flatbed truck several feet away. He cautiously grabs the bag from her hand and sets it down, then lifts her up onto the back of the truck. They look up at the stars again almost in unison. I wish it is me having a romantic moment rather than Debbie, but I'm not going to let it ruin the view.

"I knew I was missing something by living in the city," Debbie states with wonder in her voice.

With her head still tilted back as she looks skyward, Tim moves a strand of hair from her cheek, places it behind her ear, and runs his fingers along her jawbone.

"You're beautiful," he says, running his hand down her arm and scooting himself closer to her.

"You know I'm right here, right? Jeez! Get a room!"

Tim and Debbie look at each other, and he laughs as he jumps down. Debbie turns her face up toward the sky again.

I walk to the front of the house. Tim comes toward me and rustles for a key above the screen door. With a gentle thud on the dirt, it falls to the ground in front of my feet. I pick it up and hand it to him.

He and I walk through the door together. He flips on the light to reveal a large living room with two doors on the far wall. A well-used, upholstered rocking chair sits facing a huge flat-screen TV in the corner. In the opposite corner is a card table, obviously both a dining table and a fire hazard, stacked with multiple papers. The floor is hard wood, but covered in elaborately decorated area rugs.

Although the room is small, it's clean and has a little-old-lady quality about it. Except for the TV. That is certainly bachelor pad charm.

"The bathroom is over there," he says, pointing to the door on the right.

Debbie walks in and looks around like she's just stepped into a new hall of the natural history museum. She smirks. I wonder what she's thinking about.

"Bathroom is there? Is that what you said?" She walks toward the door as Tim gives a positive response.

I figure I'm getting the couch so throw my bag there and sit to take off my shoes. My stomach is killing me.

Tim smiles his fantastic smile at me and disappears into door number one.

Chapter Seven

"BREAKFAST IS READY." Tim's voice, followed by the sweet smell of syrup, is the glorious awakening I receive. He leaves quickly through a small door.

I love the quaintness of the place. It is everything Debbie and I never had. I'm not sure how I feel about that. *Will Dad be like this? Or will he be like Mom, disorganized and wild?* I sigh, get up, and reach for a clean shirt. Debbie walks past me, pulling out a cigarette, "Good morning."

She looks more relaxed than she seemed yesterday. Debbie opens the door to outside, and the cool freshness of the morning sweeps its way into the room. Almost timed with Debbie's exit, Tim enters, "Grandma's waiting. You'll want all your taste buds for the pancakes she's made."

He speaks gently, in contrast to the bold coffee

aroma wafting through the air. He crosses the room to head outside. Shortly, they both come back in, walking very close to each other, as if they are trying to cuddle and walk. I'm jealous. I'm not jealous Debbie got Tim but that I can't be in love and open about it too, walking and cuddling for everyone to see.

Leonard knows I'm in love with him. He had told me once that maybe one day we could be together, but the time was never right. It hurt that we couldn't walk around holding hands. We haven't even kissed each other. I wish we had. I dreamt about it. I know he's older than me and all my friends, but I don't care. Mom doesn't appreciate him. I wonder if Leonard's distance with me is because he is protecting Mom. He hasn't texted since the last time we spoke—when he confused me with what he said. He said it's over. He made it seem like it was my fault. My stomach hurts. I wish he would call.

Debbie looks at me, "Let's find this breakfast."

Debbie peers around the door to the kitchen like an intruder trying not to be noticed. She opens it slowly, making sure to not bump anything.

"Hello, dear!" A pleasant motherly voice calls to us. Debbie pushes the door open and we step into the kitchen. The woman smiles at us while wiping her hands on her baby-blue-and-white apron. The shiny silver clasp that holds it around her neck looks like a piece of jewelry, and my guess is that it's probably the closest thing to jewelry she ever wears. Her face is as beautifully wrinkled as a holiday dress made of crushed velvet.

She is a simple farmer's wife, one who doesn't fuss with makeup and fashion or primping. She still has an elegance about her, though, that makes me suspect she was an attractive young woman decades earlier.

The sun is shining through the window above the sink, highlighting gold and red streaks woven into her gray hair. More of her exquisite rugs are below our feet, and handmade doilies hang off the hutch against the wall.

Tim's grandmother reminds me of the way I feel with Mrs. Flanagan, longing for the grandma I never knew. Her warm, bony hand takes mine and leads me to the table, in front of a place setting. Debbie and Tim sit down at the other white plates framed with silverware, a paper napkin, and a glass of orange juice. The old woman ladles warm syrup into a spouted bowl, and Tim forks the pancakes onto his plate. Debbie follows suit, and I am eager to do the same. I wipe butter generously over each pancake, then pour the syrup on top, watching as the gooey concoction runs down the side of the stack.

Tim looks at us both and smiles. "Thank you, Grandma."

She walks over to him and kisses his cheek, then leaves us alone in the kitchen.

Tim motions to the pancakes, picks up his fork, and cuts a triangle into the stack. He sticks a bite of all four pancakes into his mouth at once. Debbie eats more heartily than I've seen her do ever before; shoving bacon and pancakes into her mouth as though it is the first meal she's had in a lifetime. She gulps down some fresh orange juice, then sits back as though signifying her satisfaction.

"So, what's in Colorado?" Tim says, breaking the breakfast mega-binge.

"That's where our dad is. We think."

"Wow. That's a bold move. Going on a road trip and not even really knowing if you will find what you're looking for." With bacon in his mouth, he adds, "What makes you think he's there? Like, what's your plan?"

Debbie and I sit quietly. *Our plan? Our plan is ridiculous. Show up somewhere near where we think our dad is and hope to bump into him. We have no plan.*

"We don't really have one," Debbie confesses, to my surprise. Actually, Debbie never worries about looking like a fool. She has no problem admitting she doesn't know things…like I do.

"What do you mean? You just hit the road with hope?" Tim sets down his fork.

"Yes," Debbie tells him. "We didn't really feel there was much of an option."

We all sit quietly again. I can almost hear Tim thinking, then he says, "What do you know about him? How have you tried so far to find him?"

I look at Debbie, not interested in much more than my pancakes and how quickly I can devour them to get the nausea out of my belly and the disgusting taste out of my mouth.

"We don't know much. We thought we had his

last name, but when we were packing, we found out that our last name is actually our mom's maiden name. We're not sure if they were ever married. We thought they met in high school, but we aren't sure about that either now."

Tim reaches for more bacon, his eyebrows push together as though he's seriously contemplating what was said.

I add, "I tried looking online, but that was before we knew his real name." My input seems pretty lame at this point.

Tim brushes his bangs off his forehead, "Well, my cousin works at the police department. He also did a little bit of PI work in the past. Maybe I can ask him to help."

Debbie and I look at each other. Our silent communication says something like, "Really? Could we really find him?"

"When we are done here, I'll have you guys write down everything you know. I'll call him and see what else he might need."

Neither of us considered using an authority to our benefit. Debbie and I have a mild distrust of the police. Okay, unhealthy distrust. I guess people who have had the police help them out, or administer justice, may think to go to them and ask for help. But kids like Debbie and me just know them as intruders. We don't answer their questions, because Mom told us they are looking for ways to trap our words and make us believe they are helping just long enough to turn the tables and prove our guilt to the world. They are there to take away rights, privacy, and security and to enforce their own authority, rules, and caged "safety."

Tim sits back in his chair and lets out a small laugh, "Are you finished or would you like more? I don't think I've seen such a small girl pack away so many pancakes!"

He looks genuinely pleased rather than disgusted at my behavior. Debbie laughs, then stands and pushes the chair in. Still giggling, she grabs a few plates and carries them over to the sink. Tim stands to put away the butter and syrup. Debbie turns on the water and begins rinsing the dishes. Tim can't keep his eyes off her. She must notice because she turns toward him, "What?"

"You are beautiful," he says. I stand up and leave.

✳ ✳ ✳

Debbie and I are playing rummy, killing time and letting our food digest. Our list was finished for Tim just after breakfast. It is well after lunch now, and we are enjoying not being in a car, not worried about our money or where we're going next. Just relaxing in a peaceful place with a nice guy.

I burp and gag at the taste of charcoal that comes up. "Yuck!"

"What?" Debbie asks. "You should see the look on your face right now!"

"I just burped this nasty charcoal taste." I wipe my face with the back of my hand.

"Yeah, they give you charcoal when you over-dose...to help absorb the toxins." Debbie looks down at her cards. "My friend Jen went through that once and told me *all* about it."

"Umm." I groan, not sure what else to say.

Debbie taps the cards on the table. She seems un-comfortable, and so am I. I don't want to talk about this. I'd rather pretend like none of it happened.

"You know," Debbie starts shuffling, "I never ex-pected you would go into my bag. That you would open that container."

I look at her blankly. *What do I say?*

"You were stupid to take pills from a bottle not knowing what they were."

"I assumed they were aspirin. I've never seen any-thing else...like any other drugs...to know the differ-ence." I feel stupid and naïve and like a little kid. "I'm sorry."

"You don't need to apologize," Debbie pushes her hair behind her ear. "It was my mistake. I'm just glad you are okay."

"Yeah, I'm okay. I'm really okay." I say it to make her feel better. She seems upset, and I don't want a fight... or this conversation. The morning has been going really well.

Debbie jumps up, "You know what? To make it up to you, I'm going to flush it all."

Ha! That would be great! But then I realize I don't really trust that she can do it. *If it were that easy to give them up, why wouldn't she have done it long be-fore now?*

She seems giddy, excited, inspired. "No, really. Here we are on this epic trip to find our dad...a new beginning...to start over with new, fresh lives. So... let's flush it. Really."

She grabs my hand and drags me to her bag, reaching in the duffle and swishing her hand around the inside until she hits the bottle and pulls out the bottle triumphantly. "Here!" she declares and whisks me toward the bathroom.

Standing over the toilet together, I laugh nervously. "Remember the funeral we had for Frankie, my goldfish?"

"Yeah, I remember. You made me and Mom wear dresses!"

We laugh together for a moment. I wonder. *If Tim were to walk in right now what would he think of us standing over a toilet giggling?*

"Well Rachel, just as we flushed Frankie in his death, let's now flush this shit and declare it dead." She says it resolutely, a note of somberness in her voice. It is truly a grief-filled event for her, as great as the passing of a goldfish was for me. Probably more. I don't know. I have never understood.

We watch the pills drop into the water, swirl, and then disappear. Debbie's face drops in sadness rather than relief, and she heads outside for a cigarette.

✳ ✳ ✳

"So, when should we leave?" Debbie asks me.

"I don't know. Do you think we'll actually find Dad?"

"I'm not sure. And how long do we wait for Tim to find him? I mean, staying here is nice, but we can't stay forever."

"No, but we still don't know what we're walking into, showing up in Colorado with nothing to go on and no place to stay." I set down a card and draw another. A two of clubs, it's worthless in this hand. "Tim said it would be just a few days to get the birth certificates. We should at least wait until then. They will be good to have."

"I'm good with that. And I can tell you being away from Mom has been good for me. I'll do whatever to start a new life without her." She picks up my discard and lays down all her cards, "Rummy and cigarette break."

I look around the room as I sit alone. I'm torn. As much as I want something new, a fresh start, I hate change. I hate the unknown. I hate not having a plan. And I hate relying on Debbie.

* * *

"Okay." Tim says, plopping down in the chair next to where Debbie and I are in the middle of our hundredth card game since we started playing four days ago.

"Okay what?" Debbie asks.

"We think we found your dad."

"What?" Debbie's jaw drops open. I'm in shock, not quite sure what I heard.

"Well, my cousin Lucas looked up some things based on what you told me, but it was actually your birth certificates that made the difference." He chuckles and continues, "Isn't life like that? Here you were looking for him...for who he is and what his characteristics would be...but completely overlooking how he relates to you. His name is on your birth certificates. It was right there, plain as day, Lucas said, and from there, your dad was super easy to find."

I'm not sure if I'm awake or dreaming right now. Literally, an hour ago we didn't have a clue how to find him. This feels so surreal. I've been experiencing this feeling a lot this past week. If my belly wasn't so full, I think I might pass out.

Tim looks excited and energized, as though it is his own personal triumph. "His name is James Donald Fraser. His last known address is in Golden, Colorado. He has a listed phone number." He pauses and looks at both of us. "Now what?"

"Are you serious?" Debbie asks.

"Should we try calling him?" Tim questions.

Debbie and I look at each other. We have never been this close. I can't find words to speak. *What if we actually really find him? I mean, that's the goal, isn't it? But it's so...so real now. Will things be better with him? Or worse? What if he doesn't want us to come? Will we turn around and go back to Cleveland?* I'm feeling overwhelmed with choices I never had before.

"Rach?" Debbie looks toward me, snapping me out of my head for a moment. She tilts her head slightly, "What do we have to lose?"

A phone is in her hand. I won't know any answers to my questions until we make that call. I grab Debbie's wrist and squeeze it. She dials the number.

"Wait!" I say, "What should we say?" I want to write a script. Debbie hits send, then the speaker button. It is so silent, I can hear my heart beating in my ears.

"Hello. You have reached Don Fraser. If you have received this message, I can't answer. If you need assistance, you may call my office at 303…"

I grab a pencil and write down the number. Adrenaline floods my body. I can't believe we're this close to talking to our dad and hearing his real voice! It feels like falling in love! Like winning a prize. Like hearing your name called over the loud speaker, "Rachel White. Rachel White, please make your way to the stage. You have just been chosen as this year's Prom Queen."

Debbie is already dialing. She almost drops the phone in excitement.

"DF Contractors. How may I help you?" A flat female voice answers.

"Um, hi, is Donald Fraser there?" Debbie says giddily.

"No, he's not. Would you like his voicemail?" the woman says with a tone of impatience.

"Well, I really need to talk to him. Do you know when he will be in?" Debbie's face drops.

"No. Would you like his voicemail?"

"This is urgent." Debbie almost pleads. We hear a click and the beginning of a voicemail box message.

"What was that about?" I ask.

"I don't know, but she was a bitch!" Debbie responds.

We look at Tim. He shrugs. "She isn't very nice. Maybe I can try?"

"Maybe it's a sign. Maybe Dad doesn't want to see us or meet us. Why would he have such a rude secretary?" I can't believe that the kind, generous man I want my dad to be would have someone so mean represent him.

"She could be having a bad day…or just be doing her job like she's supposed to." Tim responds. "Let me try."

He takes the phone from Debbie.

"No!" Debbie says, then pauses. "No, let's just wait."

All our excitement is gone. She must be feeling it too—wanting change and yet not wanting it at the same time. Wanting someone to love, someone who will love us back, but not wanting to risk the rejection. I watch her stand up and head outside. I follow.

The weather is still beautiful, and the smell of the air is clean and grassy. The only sounds I hear are my own footsteps. Quiet. I breathe in heavily, hoping to pull the peace and silence inside.

I drop to the ground next to Debbie. We sit for a moment, enjoying the soundlessness, when Debbie says, "Soon we will be at Dad's. You will see how crazy Martha really is then. I can start over. Dad will make things okay." She pauses, as the wind blows quietly on our faces, as though Nature is sighing with us.

"And if not, we will have other options. As long as we are together we don't need anyone else."

Yeah, and as long as Debbie doesn't mess up again.

Debbie continues, "Let's try Dad again tonight. And let's leave in the morning."

"Which way will we go? To Dad's or back to Mom's?"

"I don't ever want to go back to Mom's." Debbie tosses away her cigarette butt.

"Okay," I say, still unsure. Still unsure who to trust.

Chapter Eight

THE KITCHEN TABLECLOTH is mesmerizing. The light blue pattern runs from left to right and is distracting me from wiping down the table while Debbie does our breakfast dishes. Our plan today is to leave by ten, which is about twenty minutes from now. The car is already loaded. Debbie and I got ready this morning almost in complete silence.

We still hadn't gotten ahold of Dad, and I'm feeling unsure about our departure for Colorado. I think Debbie must be feeling the same way. We are both moving rather slow, enjoying the time we have been ignoring the real world. This is what home should feel like. I toss the sponge into Deb's soapy dishwater.

A few bubbles jump up and land on her shirt, and she turns and smiles at me. For a moment, our silent communication whispers, "Hope. Hope. Everything is okay."

Our smiles linger even after Tim comes into the kitchen. His smile and confidence seem silly. Maybe he lives in this place of peace and isn't just experiencing it for a short moment on a bright morning like Debbie and me.

He crosses his arms, leans back against the wall and proclaims, "I talked to your dad this morning."

"What?" Debbie asks, her eyebrows up, her arms crossing.

His face drops at her response. "I called him while you were eating. I told him what was going on. I asked him if there was anything I could do to help."

Debbie stares at him with a look I don't recognize.

Tim, as though working himself out of a hole, adds, "I wanted to make sure everything was up and up before you left me," he stops, pauses, then continues, "before you take off on some wild goose chase."

Debbie's face is frozen.

I want to ask a million questions. *What is he like? Does he want to see us? Is he excited?* Instead, I stay quiet.

"If it's okay with you and Rachel, he'd like me to come with you. He said he'd pay for my bus ticket home."

Debbie methodically turns to the dishes and pulls the plug for the water to drain. Then, like a snake as it recoils and springs to attack, she turns to Tim and screams, "I don't need a goddamn savior!"

"Debbie," he approaches her cautiously, "Your dad was concerned about his daughters, two young women, driving across the country alone. I offered to drive with you the rest of the way home. I promised him I would be a gentleman, and he said he would appreciate it and pay me for my time. That's all."

She storms past him and I follow, not quite sure if we are walking out the door forever and leaving Tim behind. I know this pattern, and even without thinking, I play my part and move mechanically through the door, following Debbie like the countless times I followed Mom.

I want to ask what we are doing. I want to know what I should do. I feel helpless. I feel useless. As Debbie pulls her cigarettes out of her pocket, I remember I need my toothbrush and jog to the bathroom to retrieve it. I peer around to make sure we have everything. I feel frantic, like I might forget something. My mind is busy with my list. The List shows up in my head whenever my heart races. The List puts everything in order and keeps the emotions silenced. Repeating The List gives me focus. Like Mrs. F's Post-its.

Toothbrush. Toothbrush. Toothbrush. Other words are buzzing around in my head, but Toothbrush is louder. I pick it up and check inside the cupboards and under the sink and around the shower stall for anything else we might have forgotten. I check again a second time. And a third. Then I check the bedroom. Under the bed. In the closet. The living room. Under the bed again. Under the couch. Near the TV.

Through the window, I see Tim and Debbie standing by the car, talking. As I watch them embrace, my heart rate slows down and returns to normal. *We aren't running away, right? Does this mean we are staying here? Are we still going to Dad's?* I run back to the couch and grab the cards to make it look like I'm playing solitaire and not spying on them. Tim walks in and plops down in his rocking chair. I shuffle the cards and start laying them out. I wish he wasn't looking at me.

"Are you okay with me going to Colorado with you guys?"

My mouth is dry, and I wish I had a piece of gum. "I don't care."

It's true, I don't. I don't know why Dad wants him to come. I don't know if I believe Tim actually talked to him, but I also don't believe he would lie.

"Tim, did he ask to talk to us? Does he want to see us?"

I swallow hard and look down. I only want to hear one answer, but I suspect the other. My heart aches as I wait for the response that is taking too long to come. Tears begin to drop as the seconds pass. His silence tells me what I already know: Dad doesn't want us.

I look up, and Tim is standing there with his arms outstretched, a look of sadness on his face. He is so welcoming, but I am shaking from the pain. All of a sudden, thin yet muscular arms wrap themselves around me. Tim squeezes me and lifts me up into a standing position. I sob into his chest. He grabs my chin and tilts it up to face him. I can barely open my eyes; they're so heavy with tears. I can't imagine how much fluid is running down my face.

"Look at me. Open your eyes," He instructs and I obey.

"Your dad is thrilled and nervous, just like you."

I wipe my nose with my shirt. I don't believe him.

He continues, "He loves you more than you know."

I feel sick with emotion. I wipe my nose again, this time with a tissue Tim hands me.

"I ask again, Rachel, because I won't go if you don't want me to. Do you mind if I go to Colorado with you?"

I shake my head. I don't mind and I might even like him. I don't trust him yet, though.

Tim smiles and picks up the duffel bag he packed. "Let's get going then!"

✳ ✳ ✳

"Look at *that* house—isn't it great?" Debbie shouts.

"That one there?" I point out toward a field.

"Yes!"

"Why do you like that one?"

"I don't know. Look at all the land around it. It looks so peaceful."

"Deb, it looks so alone. Not peaceful. Ready to fly out of control."

"What?"

"It looks like it would be the first in the path of a tornado to be swept up into nowhere. A tornado house! Perfect for a trip to Oz," I chuckle at my cleverness.

"That's a country house, Rachel. That's what they look like."

"No, a country house is beautiful. Standing tall along an unpaved road. Two stories with a big porch and a mailbox out front. That's a country house. You like a *tornado* house."

"Actually," Tim cut in, "a country house is just any house not in the city."

I glare at him.

Tim swallows hard, "Sorry. You are both right. A country house is very romantic, and I just blew it." He turns his head to look out the window.

Debbie and I laugh. Tim looks toward us again and smiles. I eye him, wondering more about him, including what he must think of us. Us two girls, ending up in his life like an explosion. As much as we have been through in the last few days, we dragged him right into it. And he's taking it all in stride. As if we are just like every other set of teenage sisters in America.

"So, Tim, I know so little about you. Tell me about yourself." I say it somewhat mockingly, but really don't mind getting to know him a bit and passing the time.

"What do you want to know?"

"Do you have a reason for taking this trip, other than Debbie?"

"Rachel! Hush!" Debbie reaches over and swats at me.

"Really, Tim, you've been dead silent for the past half hour. There must be something to talk about."

"What would you like to know then?"

"Let's start with…" I think, trying to decide which of the hundreds of questions I have in my mind to lead off with. I go straight to the heart of the matter. "Have you ever been in love?"

He pauses, pushes his hair back, "I think so, once."

"Who was she? And what happened?" I sit wide-eyed, waiting. Debbie is staring straight ahead at the road.

"Miss Carlie Payton. Her family moved away to Boston in June of my sophomore year."

"And you were in love with her?" I ask again, hoping he will elaborate.

"I think so." His eyes move as he thinks, then he asks, "Have you ever been in love?"

I'm surprised. *Can I really answer that? No way.* I just want his input, not for him to ask me.

Debbie laughs then interrupts, "Rachel is in love with her ponytail and journal."

"Shut up!" I say it playfully, thankful for the rescue.

Debbie continues the questioning, "Okay, how about, what's your favorite food?"

"Pizza!" I answer loudly.

"Steak and gravy. Not always together though," Tim answers.

Debbie takes a minute, then responds, "Cheetos. The crunchy kind. I can eat a whole bag."

＊ ＊ ＊

We pull into the gravel road that leads us to a campground. Despite the summer months, it doesn't look too terribly full. We had passed right by a campground earlier with all kinds of signs about being for families—which basically means they have a playground and kids will be screaming from sun up to well after their sundown s'mores.

Debbie registers us and pays while Tim and I unload camping gear from the trunk. It's a warm, clear day and the night promises to be pleasant and not too cold.

"It smells so good out here. I love the smell of campfires and evergreen trees," Tim says, stretching his long arms behind his head. I smile. I like that too. It's pretty much the smell of camping. And the smoke smell stays on you—on your clothes and your skin—until it's washed away.

There is a couple in a trailer across the way from us. They must be professional campers, retirees maybe. They have a picnic table set up with a huge tarp under it, lights strung over the awning, and a cooking cart fully stocked with dishes, pans, and utensils, as though they are permanently home.

To the left of us is another couple, tenting like us. I can't see their faces—they sit in lawn chairs under the sun that's beginning to set rather than beneath the shade of the large tree beside them. Their fire is roaring, obviously in preparation for the night ahead.

Debbie's approaching footsteps are followed by the sound of a cracking branch above me. A squirrel runs by frantically. "All set," Debbie says as she pulls a large duffel from the back of the car and then slams the trunk shut.

We had stopped along the way for campfire items and more ice, since we'd left Tim's house with an empty cooler. Now, the hotdogs are on sticks, waiting to take their place on our plates beside our Fritos. Of course, the marshmallows will come out a bit later. Tim sits on a stump, and Debbie and I sit in the lawn chairs we packed. It has been mostly small talk and silence, which is nice. Relaxing, non-conflict is the way to spend a night in the wilderness.

Tim speaks over the crackling fire, "Would you rather have a bear come into your tent or a skunk?"

Debbie laughs, then pulls her hotdog back to check its doneness.

I answer, "A skunk, because it doesn't necessarily have to spray—it might wander back out. Or maybe I could shoo it away nicely. A bear...I would lose my mind over a bear."

I think about it a little more. *Yeah, I'm good with my answer.* "I hope I never see either, though."

Tim and Debbie laugh. The faceless couple tenting next to us is walking beside our campground. "Nice night," the taller one says.

"Yes, it is!" Tim responds. "We have extra marshmallows. Would you like to come join us?"

They walk in our direction. As they approach, the light from the fire illuminates their faces. They are young, like in their twenties, a guy and girl, both fit in nylon pants and hiking boots. They don't necessarily match—like they aren't wearing matching Hawaiian shirts or anything like that, but their genderless outfits came from the same REI store, for sure. They look like they are made for each other.

Tim reaches out his hand, "I'm Tim." He shakes the man's hand, and the young man introduces himself as Loom. His brown hair is dreadlocked and pulled back into a ponytail. His arm is covered by a waterproof jacket, but a tattoo peeks out as he extends his arm to Tim. I look at his other exposed skin and at his neck. A shadow of a tattoo loops up from his collar. Loom introduces the female with him as "his partner, Tiff."

Really? Loom and Tiff? Annoying. Annoying dirty people that hopefully don't stick around.

Debbie bounces over to the two and shakes their hands, "I'm Debbie. This is my sister, Rachel."

She waves her arm toward me like she wants me to take a bow. I smile a fake smile and look down at my journal, barely visible with my small flashlight. *Now I have to be freaking friendly. I just want to be alone.* I'm grouchy from all the driving.

Debbie walks in my direction, a stick in her hand already loaded with two fat marshmallows.

"Hey, what's going on?"

I keep jotting nothings into my journal and roll my eyes. She asks again, "What's up?"

"Loom and Tiff? Really? Do they need to hang around?"

"Why not? Is this your forest? Your campground?"

"Kinda. This is our spot, yeah." I say. It sounds pretty snotty, but I'm annoyed. "I don't want those freaks hanging out with us."

Debbie leans back, crosses her arms, "Freaks? They haven't said more than their names."

"Yeah, freak names. Is Loom an Indian or something? What kind of name is that? And you know Tiff isn't the name her parents gave her. She's a freaking wanna-be."

Debbie's eyebrows are pressed down towards her nose. "Wow. Well, everyone can't be as perfect as Rachel White. You seriously think complete strangers need to live up to your expectations in life? They don't give a lick about what you think of them."

I don't care. I turn the page in my journal, wishing the conversation was over.

"Are you gonna sit here and be miserable because other people are cramping your style, or are you gonna come over and roast some marshmallows and have some fun? Fun, Rachel. Fun!"

I sigh. It's just not the way I planned it. I was going to Dad's on my own. Then Debbie wants to go. Now we picked up Tim. And here we sit having to interact with strangers. I stand up and walk to the fire.

✳ ✳ ✳

The morning is crisp and beautiful, as it should be. Debbie wakes up with me and we sneak out of the tent, leaving Tim zipped up behind us.

"Bathroom!" Debbie and I whisper almost in unison.

"Rachel, Tim told me he has money for a hotel room tonight. That will be nice, to have a nice hot shower. Especially after camping and then being in a car all day."

"Yeah," is my simple reply. "That will be nice." I hadn't told her about the money I'd taken from my savings. She probably would have stolen it if she'd known.

"Speaking of nice...Loom and Tiff were pretty cool."

I roll my eyes, "Yes, Debbie. They were nice." I say it mockingly. Truth be told, they *were* pretty cool. Tiff is a painter. I let her read a few of my poems. She said they were good, but everyone usually does.

Loom was funny. He made fun of his name, saying his parents were hippie "tapestry and rug makers" and felt nothing was more magical than the tool that created such woven masterpieces, like how each of us is woven together as we are woven in our mother's wombs. We all laughed when he stood and twirled his hands toward the sky in a silly "stoned fairy" voice, as Debbie put it.

And I *did* have fun. Unplanned. With Strangers.

✻ ✻ ✻

A vacancy sign glows brightly in the dark night sky. I'm exhausted. Tired of not being where we intended. Tired of being on our way to somewhere unknown. The neon buzzes as Debbie steps out and walks into the hotel office. I watch Tim studying Debbie's every move. He obviously likes her. I wonder if Leonard has ever looked at me that way. Or if he ever caught me looking at him like that. Probably not.

Debbie always has more luck with guys than I do. I don't understand why. Debbie is always unkempt, reeks of smoke, and has a bad attitude. I am attractive and polite; I shower and take care of myself. And here is Tim worshipping Debbie. Debbie is a spoiled brat. She always has been. When she didn't want to live at home, she just left. When she wanted money, she just took it. Now, she meets a guy, and after less than a week, he loves her.

Tim looks over at me and smiles, as though he knows I am thinking about him. I look away without smiling back. Tim laughs and asks, "Have you ever been to a gas station where the bathroom key is attached to a cinder block?"

He looks across the parking lot, and I follow his eyes to see what he's talking about. Debbie is over-dramatizing, pretending she is distressed by having to carry an obnoxiously large keychain for our hotel room.

I crack a smile. It is funny. Debbie throws it over her shoulder and carries it like Santa's sack. She's quite the actress. She hops back into the car, and we round the parking lot to a space on the end.

"I've got the bags." Tim declares, presumably in a show of chivalry. I jump out and snatch my bag despite his offer. Tim reaches into the trunk for the others and springs upward from the pinch Debbie places on his right butt cheek. Debbie fakes a look to her left, her hand on her forehead, her eyes squinting to see something in the dark distance. Tim cracks a smile and goes back to the bags.

Sighing loudly and rolling my eyes, I stick out my hand, "Keys, please."

Our room is the last one on the end of the U-shaped, ranch-style motel. I march down the Astroturf hall to the room, the keychain bumping my thigh. The door clicks open, and my hand rubs along the wall until my fingers finally stumble upon the light switch that lights up the small room.

Not bothering to look around, I beeline to the bathroom. I'm annoyed with Debbie and Tim who have been flirting all day. They get to flirt and fall in love and hold hands and kiss each other, and they are doing all this in front of me. I drop my backpack and just as quickly let my clothes fall to the floor as I climb into the shower, cranking it to the hottest temperature I can tolerate. The smell of the campfire smoke drips off, replaced with fresh, clean soap.

The water is almost unbearable. Sometimes, that's how I like it. I want to feel the heat on my skin, see it turn red, purge my anger. A half-hour later, I turn off the water and hear Debbie laughing loudly. I crack open the door and peek out, mostly to make sure Tim and Debbie are still dressed. Sitting on the end of the bed, watching some goofy movie on late-night TV apparently warrants lots of laughter.

I gently ease the door closed and clean the mist off the mirror, gazing at myself as it fogs up again. Grabbing a dry towel, I begin wiping the moisture off the walls. It's a compulsion I have. After my really hot showers, I wipe everything down. All the steam sanitizes things. While the droplets of water are removed from the porcelain, tile, and chrome, droplets form on my head and neck, making me pant. It's a frantic work-out and I feel high.

"Rachel. I need to get in there. Are you almost done?" Debbie knocks on the door and breaks my trance.

"Umm, yes, just a second." Standing naked with my hands on my hips, breathing in deeply, I lower my heart rate. I pull on a pair of fuzzy pajama pants and undershirt from my bag, toss it over my shoulder, and open the door for Debbie.

The bed is cool and relaxing. But my stomach is still not right. Leonard is not returning my texts. I wonder if Mom's still in her hospital bed or in the rehab facility yet. I wonder how upset Patricia will be if we don't succeed in making it to Dad's. Almost simultaneously, these thoughts pass through my mind. *Does my brain ever quiet? Is it possible that one day it will spin right out of my head?*

I hear the bathroom door pop, followed by the movement of the bed as Debbie climbs in beside me, giving Tim the other free bed.

"Do you want this bed? I can sleep on the floor," he asks.

"No," Debbie whispers, "This is fine." The light shuts off. I hear shuffling and the bathroom door shut. Debbie whispers to me, "Rachel. I don't believe you are asleep yet. I just want you to know I love you and I'm sorry."

I keep my eyes closed. I don't know where that came from or why she needed to say it now. I don't reply and try my best to fall asleep for real.

Chapter Nine

THE WAITRESS SETS three hot cups of coffee in front of our trio. Breakfast is pretty much the only meal sustaining us. The road trip allows us all kinds of snacks that we grab at gas stations along the way, creating a "grazing" habit that doesn't require the three-sit-down-meals-a-day routine.

"We should be able to make it to Dad's by tonight." Debbie pronounces, folding up the map.

Neither Tim nor I say anything. I'm not feeling very well. A mop bucket props one of the bathroom doors open, and the strong smell of cleaner lingers in my nose, making me even more nauseous.

Debbie dials the number Tim jotted down for her. Without reservation, but still with a bit of her attitude, she asks, "Don? Donald? Uh, Dad? This is Debbie."

She moves the phone from her mouth, blows out

a sigh, and rolls her eyes at me. I guess that didn't go the way the tough girl planned. I sip my coffee. She matter-of-factly communicates where we are and furiously scribbles down directions.

"Okay. Yeah, I will call if I have any trouble," she nods and smiles at me. "We are fine. Yes, the trip has been fine. Okay. Okay. Bye."

She sets the phone down and grabs her coffee. "All ready."

She's smiling, beaming even, as our plates are placed on the table. I'm pushing food around my plate. I want to eat, but I just can't stomach it.

"I'm going to wait in the car."

✳ ✳ ✳

I'm seated in the backseat with my arms crossed, when Debbie jumps into the passenger seat. Tim takes the cue and drops himself into the driver's seat. He pushes the seat back before starting the car. As he adjusts the mirrors, he catches my unfriendly eyes. I'm glaring at him, but he seems not to notice. He reverses and asks, "Which way?"

I sigh.

"West," Debbie points to the highway sign, "Right there." Tim flips on the blinker and turns. I grab a grocery bag that's on the floor and fling it open so that it pops open against Tim's head. I bend down and begin to pick up the small pieces of French fries and wrappers that made their way to the floor.

"Why do you keep everything such a mess, Debbie? You live like a slob." I'm irritable. I don't feel good and I want to fight.

"What the hell are you talking about, Rachel? The car is fine."

"Look at this! Look at all the crap on the console. Do you ever wipe it off?"

"What is your problem? Seriously Rachel!"

"Nothing. You're just a pig, that's all."

"That's not what I asked." Debbie gives me a look and I get quiet. Crossing my arms again, I drop back into the seat. I turn my head so I don't have to look at her. She questions me anyway, "I saw how you always kept your room more organized than a drill sergeant at Mom's house. And I know you cleaned the bathroom last night. What's wrong with you? Do you have OCD? Or are you just a bitch? What the hell?"

I continue to look out the window. I can feel Debbie looking at me, waiting for a response. Getting my icy silence, Debbie turns around in her seat and looks out front. Tim looks at me in the reflection again. I don't meet his eyes. He reaches forward and turns up the radio.

Debbie turns back to me. "And I hate closed shower curtains. I thought you knew that, Rachel. Your little shower stunt last night freaked me out."

I look at her with a puzzled expression. *How would I know that? What is she talking about?*

She chews on her index fingernail and then starts talking. "I woke up one morning to get ready for school. The bathroom door was closed, but I didn't think anything of it. I was still pretty tired, was gonna turn the radio on, but reached into the shower first to get the water started. That's when I saw her foot and the red water she was laying in. I was sure she was dead. I ran right to the phone to call 9-1-1. I couldn't go back in there. They wanted me to check her pulse, to see if her head was above water, but I couldn't. I lit a cigarette and waited for the paramedics to arrive."

Tim places his hand on her leg, "I'm sorry."

"They told me she'd passed out from her medications. They had to warm her up because her temperature was really low. I was sure she was dead. I still can't stand closed shower curtains. I cringe when I need to open them. I spent a week talking to police, social workers, and nurses. I spent the following weekend crying instead of hanging out with my friends. I don't have any tears left to cry—not for her, not for anyone. She took them all. I can't get the image out of my head."

We are all silent. The air is still. I don't think Debbie cares about life anymore. I feel that way sometimes too. I mean, think about the insanity that set us off on this trip. Mom slicing herself up again. The blood. That stain that kept spreading. I didn't know about Debbie's experience. The difference is I stayed while she ran away.

"Oh, I love this song." Debbie pronounces and bends to turn it up more.

"Me too!" Tim announces, "Do you remember when this song came out?" He smiles.

"Yeah, I was in eighth grade. Me and my friend Kristen used to lip sync to it on her front porch." Debbie shifts her body around to the beat, and Tim watches her and the road, looking amused.

"It's too bad this was their only hit, huh?" Tim laughs. I throw myself forward, shooting my arm towards the radio, and twist the knob so the volume goes all the way down.

"I'm in love with Leonard!" I blurt out. I actually shout it. It's out and I am shaking. I'm exhilarated, scared, and sick all at once.

Debbie and Tim turn to look at me. Tim snaps back to watch the road and begins to ease over to the shoulder. Debbie turns completely around in her seat.

"*What?*" she asks.

"I knew you wouldn't understand." *Oh my god, is she ever going to listen to me?* I'm so frustrated. I just want to be heard. I want her to hear me and not laugh. I feel tears forming.

"No. Please, continue. I'll listen." Debbie says with a somber expression and a slow, low, serious tone.

"We made plans to be together."

Debbie sits still; her lips open like she is going to say something or is in shock. "Did you guys…did you guys *do* anything?" A quizzical look is on her face.

I look at her, unsure what she means. "You mean kiss?"

"Uh, yeah, that *or anything else?*"

I smirk and tilt my head, thinking of what *that* would be like. "No. We were waiting until we left."

I dreamt of that day so many times. Played out how it would go, how it would feel to finally be free to express myself with him, to not hide anymore. Then I remember and tell them, "But then, when all this happened, he told me we weren't going to go away together…that it was all wrong. And I don't know what he meant."

I can't get my thoughts straight. All the confusion is coming back in. "He rejected me. I love him and he won't return my calls."

I start to cry, and my nose is running. I can tell they don't understand. I need to pull it together. They are both silent, so I change the subject. "It makes me feel better, to clean places like the bathroom. I guess I burn off bad energy when I do it…purge sort of. Sometimes, everything around me feels or looks filthy and I get a little carried away."

"I can't believe that scumbag Leonard would do that!" Debbie screams, hitting the dashboard with her hand. "I would have killed him if he touched you!"

"Debbie, it's fine." I say.

"No, Rachel, it's not okay. He is Mom's boyfriend and a grown man! It was bad enough he tried to be my dad and give me rules and discipline me like he wasn't just another man Mom had lured into her pathetic life. How did any of this start?"

I am torn by wanting to defend a man who hurt me and wanting to join in bashing him. "We would talk at night when Mom went to sleep. We would joke about what life would be like if it could be anything we could imagine. And I remember the night I said, 'Yeah, just you and me…we could be happy together.' And when I said it, I thought about it for real and knew I loved him. From there, we mostly didn't talk about it again, except every once in a while. And one time, he said maybe it could be real. I wanted it to be real, Debbie."

I am emotional again. Sad that my dream is gone. Debbie bends back over the seat and puts her arm around my neck, giving the best hug she can manage in a car. She sighs, "I'm sorry, but it could have been a lot worse. Going to Dad's is going to change a lot for us. We will have a family again. We will. You'll see."

Debbie looks at Tim. After several moments of silence, I notice my heart racing. I laugh nervously and slide my hands under my eyes to wipe the tears that have gathered and escaped to the outside corners.

"Rachel," Tim's voice is soft and soothing, "Leonard didn't reject you. He realized that planning to run away with you was a really bad idea. It doesn't have anything to do with you."

"But why?" I don't really want an answer. I just want to cry. And so I do. Uncontrollably.

Debbie gets out of the car and lights a cigarette. I don't care. Tim reaches back and puts his hand on my knee. I want to crawl into his lap and cry. After a few minutes, I am laying in the backseat. Tim and Debbie are talking. She seems upset again. She opens the door and drops into the passenger seat, then Tim drops into his seat.

"What's wrong, Debbie?" Tim asks.

"I need a cigarette."

"Okay, so have one."

"That was my last one." She opens the glove box, searching for something. I'm sure she's hoping a cigarette will magically appear.

"Okay. There will be another rest stop soon and we can stop then." Tim says reassuringly.

"Yeah. Unfortunately, that doesn't help me right now. I'm hungry and tired and we're talking about a bunch of shit I don't want to be talking about and I can't get high. So, I'm pissy right now. Can we go?" She is talking monotone, like my boring algebra teacher, but her words are stupid, like those from a stubborn, ignorant child.

"You know, Debbie, it's all about you, isn't it? You act like how you feel is all our fault. Get high, Debbie! I'm sure you have another stash hidden somewhere. Being at Dad's won't change a thing. You are still an addict. Just know I'm still crapping charcoal and my stomach hasn't been right in days. But, just like usual, take what's going on with me and make it all about you! You are so selfish!"

I don't know what guts I have to say all that. Maybe saying the truth about Leonard finally freed all these words I've been holding in for years. Maybe I have nothing left to lose. Debbie shoots me the meanest look I have ever seen. She opens her door and swings around to open mine. She grabs my feet and starts pulling me out of the car. I fight her with everything I have, twisting and grabbing for the door. Her fury and arms are strong, and as soon as my knees hit the door jam, I turn to stand rather than have my face hit the ground. I can see it in her face that she wants to hit me, but instead she turns and backs away, "You don't know what it was like for me in that house, Rachel! You act like everything is 'poor Rachel' this and that."

Debbie lunges for me, and just as quickly, Tim wraps his arms around her to hold her back, just in time to stop her assault.

"Really?" I scream back, "And you don't know what it's been like for me because you left me behind! You left me to clean up the mess. Why would you think I could handle Mom any better than you? Who was there to protect me and help me?" My throat is so dry it burns.

Debbie glares at me, "I should have had a normal Mom! I shouldn't have to shut the images down, shut my feelings down, silence the horrors of that. That's why I left."

Her eyes are wild and dry.

"Debbie," I respond slowly. "You don't need to tell me why you ran away. You are still running, and I was stuck there. You left me there to do it all alone."

She turns toward me and this time she sniffles. "I know, and then I almost killed you. You could have died because of my shit, my escape, my drugs."

She moves toward me, and Tim drops his arms. She grabs me and hugs me, "I almost killed you and I'm so sorry. I'm so sorry. I was honest back at Tim's when I flushed my shit. I flushed all of it, even what I stole from Mom when we were in the house packing. I'm so sorry. I flushed it, I promise. I swear I did. And I'm sorry."

We stand in an embrace for a long, long time. I feel like my hurt is melting and maybe Debbie's is too. She whispers to me, "I love you. Will you please forgive me?"

I pull her tighter, "Yes."

Chapter Ten

THE ROCKY MOUNTAINS are almost magical in the way they peak over the flatlands. Seeing them from a distance, they look so small, but I know how big they must actually be for me to be able to see them from where we are. I know we are still really far from Golden. I hadn't remembered how beautiful the snow-capped mountains were.

"There's home," Debbie says.

We are all quiet, as though the Rockies are the promised land, our refuge, our liberation. In reality, I have no idea if things will be any better with Dad. But I hope they will be. I didn't even recognize how much freedom I would feel by just getting away from the chaos at home. But then again, I did purge. I did let go of all the crap I was fighting to keep hidden. Like trying to hold a ball under water for sixteen years, the pressure of letting it finally surface and explode into the air was as supernatural as the mountains calling me home.

The dry, hot Denver sun beats through the windows, like being inside a tanning booth. We drive through town on I-70 for what seems like forever. Then we take an exit—not for a rest stop, but to really exit for good. To get to our destination.

Days of tears, failed planning, uncertainty, Gummy Bears, apples, and Diet Cokes is all coming to this. We are so close, and I don't know if I should cry or scream, but my stomach is in knots.

Debbie is giving instructions to Tim, who turns, looks at her, and turns again. The tension or excitement, or whatever this is, fills the car like a hot air balloon.

"I think that's it," Debbie says, pointing to an attractive, well-maintained brick house with a stone stairwell winding its way up to a porch.

Her statement is confirmed when a tall, slender, bearded man runs out toward us. Grabbing the passenger door handle, he opens it and reaches in for Debbie like a kidnapper might snatch a child from a car. I am slightly in shock to see a grown man behave with such excitement and passion. He grabs Debbie with so much force she almost falls backward. He lifts her off the ground with his embrace. Tears drop from his and Debbie's faces, and I am starting to tear up just watching them. He sets her down and nearly crawls into the backseat to get me. I'm already holding my door open to exit when he gives me the same welcome as Debbie.

His strong arms pull me up and out towards him. I feel sick for a moment as he spins me around. He smells like hair oil and cologne. I giggle, like I'm two again. It feels familiar, as if I remember him doing this before. I feel weightless and free as my legs swing off the ground.

His short beard gently scratches my face, like I'm being held by a bear. His smile nearly wraps around his face, and I look into his eyes—crystal blue and moist.

"Welcome home!" He says with such excitement and emotion, like he's wanted to say it for sixteen years. It is like a cheesy love story or Hallmark commercial, but it is real and perfect and I'm eating up every second of it.

Our dad, *our dad!* grabs our hands and pulls us toward the house. He gives Tim a head nod, acknowledging that he saw him too and indicating that Tim should follow us. Dad puts his arms around mine and Debbie's shoulders and pulls us even closer to him. We stumble over our own feet, trying to find some balance, all mashed together in a walking embrace as we move up the stairs. His enthusiasm is ridiculous yet contagious. He's saying things about dinner and the week's plans, almost speaking too quickly for us to comprehend. We are obviously at the correct house.

The house is beautiful. It is rustic, masculine, and clean, with a log cabin look and feel. It is open inside, allowing anyone to see the living room, dining room, and kitchen when you enter the house. Tim enters the foyer behind us with our bags. "Very nice," he says as he sets them on the floor.

"Dad, this is Tim," Debbie says, and they extend hands to each other. Don grabs Tim's hand and then pulls him in for a hug.

"I put you girls in a room upstairs, and Tim, I have bedding set up for you on the couch. Guys, go drop your stuff and we will get going on dinner and catching up."

I can smell the grill but don't feel hungry yet because I'm too excited. It feels unreal. I can't believe we are here.

"I just took the steaks off a while ago, so they should still be hot." He grabs a baked potato from the oven with his bare hand and throws it on the counter. He laughs, "Hot little devil!"

He snatches a hand towel hanging on the side of the sink and rescues the remaining three potatoes, setting them in a large bowl. Debbie picks up the bowl and brings it over to the dining room table. A glow of happiness surrounds her.

"Anything I can do?" I ask. Donald pauses and looks at me with an expression that makes me a little uncomfortable, like he's looking through me. Like he is amazed at my words or in love with my voice...or something.

"When I fell in love with your mom, it was partly because her voice was like a symphony. It was beautiful and melodic, whether she was speaking or singing.

You have that same voice," he pauses and his trance breaks, "Yes...there is salad in the fridge. Can you grab that please?"

I think I'm blushing. The heat moved to my cheeks. Whether or not the color changed, I don't know. "Mom doesn't sing," I say, almost under my breath. *Does she?*

"What do you mean? Of course she sings," Dad tells us. "She never sang for you? She sang the Star Spangled Banner one year for a minor league baseball game and the hairs on my arms stood on end."

Debbie and I look at each other, surprised to learn something new and lovely about our mom.

I open the refrigerator door, "I don't see the salad."

"Right there," he points. "Salad in a bag." He shrugs and makes a funny face, "Forgive me, I don't do salad too often. There's dressing in there too—on the door."

I laugh. "Should I put this in a bowl or should we just shake the lettuce out of the bag?"

Dad looks at me and smiles. I haven't had so much fun or been this silly in a long time, maybe ever. Realizing I really am hungry, I sit down at the dining room table.

✳ ✳ ✳

The grandfather clock in the dining room chimes eleven o'clock, catching us off guard. It's hard to believe it must have rung earlier and we didn't even notice.

We'd finished eating a long time ago and have been sitting in the living room, looking through pictures and sharing stories. The last pictures Dad had of us were when Debbie was in second grade. Dad said Mom stopped sending pictures after that. He had tried making contact several times, he told us.

"Your mom would tell me she had given you my info but that you didn't want to talk to me. I felt like it couldn't be true, but I didn't know what she was telling you about me. I didn't know what you believed about me, and I thought it was possible you really didn't want contact. There were times I called and she threatened me. I thought it was best to just wait until you guys searched for me."

"I'm sorry, Dad." I say, feeling bad for him.

"Sweetie," Dad says, "I didn't say that to beat up your mom, or make you feel you did anything wrong. I just want you to know I love you—I always have. I really loved your mother too. I still do. But she's not the same person I married. I had so much guilt over not being able to stay and support her, and not being able to see you guys after I left. I believed deep in my heart that one day you would look for me."

He smiles and looks down. I can tell he is holding back emotion, holding back tears. "Even though we were already separated and living apart, your mom was really upset when I told her I wouldn't move to Ohio with her. She thought it would be a fresh start for us. My business was really growing here and I thought maybe it could be good for your mom to go without me—maybe she would get some help—maybe figure some things out. I wanted you both to stay, but she knew how much it would hurt me to take you, so she did. Sometimes I wish I'd fought more, but I felt like the fight would have pushed her further into self-destruction. I couldn't do that to any of you. I just had to believe."

I want to cuddle into his lap and make everything better. I'm angry at Mom for the way she pushed Dad away. I'm also angry at myself for not looking for him sooner.

Dad takes a drink of his water, holding it in his hand as his mind seems to be searching for something, as if he's deciding whether he's said all he wants to say. His glass hits the table with a thud, "Oh! And speaking of your mother, Rachel, you need to call her tomorrow morning…please."

He pauses, looks at us both again. He is handsome, and I imagine twenty years ago that he must have been even more so. I can see why Mom chose him.

"Wow, I'm not used to being up this late! I'm beat." Donald says. "I've enjoyed this and I don't want it to end, but I need sleep."

He stands up and hugs us each. "Tim, I'm trusting you to stay here," he turns to Debbie, "And I trust you, Debbie, to stay in your own room tonight. Got it?"

They both nod.

"Dad," I say gently, getting used to hearing that

word come out of my mouth, "I'll take care of the dishes."

"Oh, we got carried away and left those out, didn't we?" He smiles and pulls me to him and kisses my forehead. "That would be great, honey, but if you're tired, we can wait until morning. Your call. Goodnight." I watch Dad climb the stairs to his room.

My choice? I've never really been given a choice before to do chores or not. I look at Debbie, "I'm going to bed."

✳ ✳ ✳

I wake before anyone else in the house. I feel like taking time while it's silent to sneak out to the back porch and sit in the sun with my journal. I carefully tiptoe down the stairs. The third one creaks, and I look behind me before I realize I don't have to fear squeaking floors here. I smile and see Tim stretched out on the couch. It is just a bit too short for the length of his body, so his ankles hang off the side awkwardly.

I slowly open the sliding door and slide only the screen closed behind me. *That way, I'll be able to hear the others as they start getting up.* There is a lovely wooden chair facing a rocky mountainside that I decide will be my basking place. I breathe in new dry smells. *Grasses or wildflowers?* I'm not sure.

I hear a noise in the kitchen behind me but keep my eyes closed, letting the sun rest on my cheeks and eyelids, warming me. I hear rustling and beeping, followed minutes later by the aroma of freshly brewed coffee.

"Good morning, sweetie," my dad's voice says to me through the screen. I smile and walk into the kitchen.

"And good morning, Tim," he says to Tim, who nods and smiles tiredly. Tim rubs his eyes as he pulls out the chair beside me at the island in the kitchen. Donald pours him a cup of coffee.

"I promised you a bus ticket back, but I haven't picked it up yet. I didn't know your plans, so I figured we'd pick them up when you were ready. I've rescheduled all my appointments this week so I can show the girls around. You're welcome to stay."

He grasps Tim's shoulder and continues, "But if you stay this week, I don't want any funny business between you and Debbie."

Tim looks at Dad, and the silent communication is some kind of warning spoken through the stern look on Dad's face.

"I understand, sir," Tim says.

Debbie appears at the top of the stairs, looking down at the two men and me in the kitchen. The look on her face is a mix of curiosity and maybe love. At least that's what it seems like as she lingers there rather than head down right away.

"Hi guys. Sleep well?" She asks once she finally descends.

"Good morning, sweetie. I've got an exciting week planned," Dad says, "And Tim will stay another day or two, if that's okay with you."

"Yeah. Yeah, that's good." She says, grabbing a cup of coffee.

"I hope you guys aren't too old for the zoo. Denver Zoo is awesome. I'd really like to take you there today. And if you don't mind, let's leave here by noon please," Dad says and kisses my forehead before he walks out of the room.

Debbie looks and me and smiles, "Is this for real?"

I smile back. "I know. It's like being on a vacation. And I don't mind the zoo, do you?"

"No, I'm happy to do anything. I'm just so glad to be here." She puts her hand on Tim's shoulder and rubs it as she sits beside him and sips her coffee.

The phone rings and we look at each other, a bit startled. Dad must pick it up in the other room, because after the second ring, it stops. Dad comes down the stairs, the receiver up against his ear, "Yes, of course…okay," he says, then extends his arm and hands the phone to me. "Ms. Aroyo wants to speak to you."

Not the way I want to start the morning. "Hello?"

"Hi Rachel! So glad to hear you made it okay."

"Yes, um, we got here last night."

"Is everything going okay?"

"Yeah, yeah, it's really good."

"Okay, well, your mom gave me the number once she realized where you guys went. Rachel, I think this could be a good move for you. But, I will need to have a local social worker do a welfare check on you and we can go from there. Sound good?"

Uck. What sounds good is not being on the phone with Patty at all right now. "Yes, that's good."

"Great. Can I talk to your father again then please?" I nod as though she can see me through the phone. "Oh, and Rachel, I'm glad you're safe. And I really hope you are happy there. Be a kid, okay?"

I don't say a thing, just hand the phone back to Dad. He jots things down on a notepad and continues his conversation with Patty.

It's not bad, really. She's not making me come back. That's good. That's really good. Next will be to talk to Mom. Maybe tomorrow.

"Got it. Okay, bye." Dad says as he hangs up the phone. Again, he extends his arm and hands me the receiver, "Call your Mom, please."

Ugh. My heart begins to race. I dial the number as Dad stands there looking at me. "You can do this. I'm here."

"Genesis Rehabilitation Center, this is Roberta, how can I help you?"

"I'm calling for Martha White please." I say, avoiding Dad's watchful eyes.

"One moment," the operator says.

I hold my breath, hoping Mom won't answer. The phone clicks and I recognize her voice, "Hello?"

"Hi Mom, I—" She cuts me off immediately.

"Rachel, I need you here." I hear shuffling noises, like she's agitated, frantically moving things around or something. "The house is a mess."

Is that why she wants me there? To clean house? How can she say that? She's not even home!

Without a pause, she continues, "Honey, you

know I need you to help me. I know your father has been telling you terrible things about me to get you to stay. He's always been that way. He's always trying to turn you girls against me."

"Mom—" I begin, but desperately, she interrupts again.

"Don't you see how evil he is? He's trying to keep you away from me."

"Mom, I'm here and I'm safe. We just got here. Yesterday, okay? There are no plans. I feel like I'm just beginning to breathe right now. Like I just learned to breathe really. That's all."

"Rachel, you are so selfish! How dare you! I've had enough of your mouth."

I hear her lighter and can picture her hand shaking as she lights her cigarette. She continues between clenched teeth, "You're with him for a night and talk to me like this? I better see you in the next few days, young lady!"

She sniffles and goes on, "You're in big trouble. I'm going to report your father for kidnapping. You just get your ass home! Did you hear me?"

"Yes, you're yelling," I say calmly. "And you won't be home for another few weeks, so I can stay at least that long."

"Smart-ass! Put him on the phone. Put Don on the phone! NOW!"

I turn to my dad, "She wants to talk to you." I put my hand over the receiver. "She's a bit hysterical," I whisper, then hand him the phone.

The phone is on his ear for less than ten seconds before he says, "Martha, I don't want to hear it."

He holds the receiver away from his ear and looks at me as the vulgarities fly across the room. Donald blushes and covers the phone to muffle the language. It doesn't stop, so he hangs up. It's not like I haven't heard it all before, and for the first time in my life, I'm not afraid. I don't feel like hiding, or running.

"I'm sorry," he says. "You didn't need to hear that." He looks blankly at me. "Are you guys ready to get out of here?"

Debbie and Tim are standing, mouths nearly agape. In unison they respond, "Yes!"

Chapter Eleven

THE OTHER DAY at the zoo was fun. Debbie pretty much ignored Tim, who kept watchful eyes on her nearly the whole time. He looked pleased, though— not jealous or bored or anything. It was nice. We've all enjoyed our time together these past few days.

Dad told us he needed to do a small job this morning and wouldn't be here when we got up, but he had plans for us later. He also said there would be a gift for us when we woke up. It is like Christmas to know I'll have a gift waiting for me.

Debbie is still asleep, so I quietly sneak out again. Sure enough, there on the stairs are two large yellow envelopes, one with Debbie's name on it and the other with mine. They are oversized mailing envelopes tied with twine, like what you would mail a t-shirt or book in. Our names are written in thick black marker.

I open my envelope and discover several folded pieces of paper and lots of greeting cards. I pour them out onto the floor in front of me. They are dated, so I open the earliest first. A dried, pressed flower is crumbled in the folds of the paper inside.

"Dear Rachel,

I love you. I know you are starting kindergarten this year. I'm excited for you! Here is a flower for your first day. Wish I was there.

Love,

Dad"

I open the next, and it is similar to the first. In fact, they are all letters from my dad for all kinds of events he wasn't there to share with me. By the third one, I am crying, a mix of smiles for the beauty of the notes and sadness at missing him. My heart hurts.

"Rachel?" I hear Debbie whisper.

I look at her from the bottom of the stairs, tears still in my eyes. Tim is asleep behind me in the living room, so she motions for me to come back up to the room. I plop down on my bed next to her.

"I don't know what to do," she says to me, like she's about to tell me a secret.

"About what?"

"Tim." She says with a silly look on her face.

I give her a look that says, "Continue" as I make circles in the air with my hand.

"Dad hasn't given us any alone time together, but we sat on the porch last night and…and I didn't know if I wanted to pounce on him and hold him for dear life or shake his hand as though nothing has changed from the first day we met."

She smiles a quirky love-struck smile. "I mean, I hardly know him, but I feel really close to him. I can feel him watching me, and when I look at him, he doesn't turn away or act like he's in some kinda peaceful trance looking off."

"Okay, so what are you thinking about? I mean, it's obvious you like him."

"I think I do." She bites her fingernail. "I asked him if he was disappointed he stayed and he said, 'No, not at all.'"

Jeez, get on with it Debbie! "Okay…and…?"

"He said, 'So where do we go from here?' You know, he's leaving today."

"Yeah, I know. And what did you say?"

"I said I don't know." Debbie picks a piece of lint from her knee.

"I've never had luck with relationships…or with men in general. Tim is great. Too great."

"Debbie? And you don't think you deserve a great guy?"

Debbie looks at me flatly. "No, it's not that. I don't want to *mess up* a great guy."

"If you really like him and let him go, how will you feel?" I like this conversation with Debbie. I feel like equals. Like I have a friend.

"Oh my gosh, Rachel! He put his hand on my face and kissed me and I thought I would explode! I wanted to stay in that kiss forever."

"And you are willing to never have that kiss again?"

"Nope. I want another one right now!" She gave me a sneaky rebellious wink.

"And send Tim home in a body bag if Dad walks in?" I laugh and she laughs with me.

"Okay, I'll get in the shower. What are we doing today?"

"I don't know," I answer, "and I don't care either!"

Debbie stands up and grabs her clothes from the floor to head into the bathroom. "And," I continue, "you need to see what Dad left for us."

✳ ✳ ✳

Debbie and Tim sit holding hands in the backseat of Dad's Explorer. Dad keeps checking the rearview mirror to make sure that's all they're doing. I'm smiling about the whole thing as we pull up to the bus station.

"Tim, I'm going to circle so you and Debbie can get out here and say your goodbyes. Rachel, why don't you get out too and keep them company? I'm going to go around once and then let's get going."

I roll my eyes. *Seriously? Dad's going to make me their stupid chaperone?*

Debbie opens the door to exit. Tim does the same, grabbing his duffel bag. Reluctantly, I hop out, and Dad drives off as a security guard waves at him to leave the drop-off zone.

The three of us stand on the sidewalk, and I take a few steps away so they can have some privacy, but also so I can still hear their conversation. Hopefully, Debbie tells him her feelings.

Tim hugs her, then presses his lips against hers. He moves his kiss to her cheek, then her neck, and slides his arm around her waist. I'm embarrassed, so I turn my back.

"Call me when you get back, so I know you're okay, alright?" Debbie says.

"Okay," He says. "Did you think more about what we talked about?"

"Yeah." Debbie replies.

"Well?"

"Yes, I'd like to give us a chance."

I feel like I just witnessed a marriage proposal or something. I've got butterflies in my stomach. I'm excited for Debbie. I turn around to see them in a hug.

Debbie is smiling the most genuine smile I have ever seen on her face.

Tim kisses her again briefly. "Well, here comes your dad, so I'm gonna go."

"Okay," she says, pushing out her bottom lip in a pout.

"And, um, next time you kiss me like that, I won't be able to leave." Tim winks at Debbie and heads inside. Debbie is beaming as he does.

Dad pulls up and we jump into the car. As soon as we are settled, Dad says, "Girls, let's get lunch and have a chat."

Debbie and I look at each other. A "chat"? I wonder what that means. Is he upset with us? Debbie must think so too, because we sit in awkward silence for several minutes.

Dad eases the Explorer into a parking space at El Sol Mexican restaurant. We get out quietly, and Debbie comes around and holds my hand as we walk in to eat.

"Three today?" The hostess asks. Dad nods. He seems serious and somber. We follow the skinny hostess to our table, where Debbie and I slide into one side of the booth and Dad into the other.

Dad doesn't pick up his menu. He just immediately says, "We need to talk about how long the two of you are staying."

I can't stand not knowing, "Dad, are you mad at us?"

"Oh, sweetie, no. I need to plan things, though… to get things in order." He pauses, looks at me, and raises an eyebrow, "Why, should I be mad at you?"

Debbie speaks up first, "It's just you were so serious."

Donald sips from his water, "Girls, the truth is, I want you to stay. I love having you around. I have a lot on my mind, though, because Martha is going to put up a fight."

A short woman with precisely applied makeup approaches our table. "You ready to order or have questions?"

Oh, I have lots of questions. None of them about the menu. Does Dad really want us to stay? How long? Will I go to school here? Will Debbie stay? What will Mom do?

Dad orders his food, and so does Debbie as I get

an elbow in my side to give my order. "Combo J," I say, and the conversation intruder walks away.

Dad continues, "I want to do what is best. Patty told me your mother will have thirty days of outpatient counseling. I don't think that's a great environment for you, but I also worry about Martha's ability to care for herself. Rachel, what do you think?"

"Well," I think out loud, "right now, I don't miss her at all. Actually, it's really nice to not have to think about any of it. It's good being with you."

Debbie chimes in, "I left Rachel to take care of Mom by herself. I could help. If we go back, I can do more."

I look at Debbie in disbelief. I would love her help. "Debbie, you left for a reason. I mean, Mom will still be crazy and Leonard will still be Leonard. It won't be any different."

"I know. But I was really selfish in leaving. I see that now." Debbie grabs my hand and squeezes. Still looking in her eyes, I announce, "I don't want to go back home. I want to stay for the summer."

"I second that!" Debbie says, raising our two hands together upward.

"I would love to have you both here, and I will do what's necessary for you to be able to stay, Rachel. In the meantime, we do need to talk about rules. We need to establish some ground rules." Our hands drop back down to our sides.

Magically, Dad pulls a pen from his pocket and opens his napkin for the impromptu writing.

Debbie stiffens. "Rules" might as well have been a cuss word to her.

"Okay. What do you guys want for rules?" Dad begins.

"What? What do WE want?" Debbie and I look at each other.

"Um, candy for dinner, pizza every Friday, no chores." I say, giggling.

Dad looks at us intently, as though he is pondering the acceptability of such a proposition. "Okay, pizza every Friday is doable. Let's work on adding some more realistic ones too. I mean, unless stomach aches and living in a filthy house are really on your list of dreams."

He looks at us both with wisdom hiding behind his pupils. His trickster eyeballs. His lovely, witty blue orbs. I speak up, "Well, I think a rule should be that we talk to each other each week about our schedules so we know what everyone is doing."

Debbie is playing with her straw. "What?"

I continue, "Well, like if you have to work, Debbie, and won't be able to do something on the weekend… or I have plans with friends and won't be home for dinner. I think we should all know those things." I look down. "Maybe it's stupid."

"Great idea. What else?" Dad asks. I can't help but beam.

Debbie takes a sip of her soda then says, "No smoking in the house."

"Great idea. That is one of my rules. I would like

you to quit entirely, because I love you and it is best for your health. But, you are eighteen, and if you must smoke, do it outside."

We named a few more rules before our food was set in front of us. "Hot plates, be careful," is all the waitress says before she walks away.

Dad rubs his hands together. "I need another napkin!" We laugh. He continues, "I will call Patty and Martha tomorrow and let them know the plan. I can't even tell you how glad and excited I am that you girls want to stay."

He sticks a forkful of enchiladas into his mouth, moans, and rolls his eyes back in his head. I giggle.

"Oh so good!" he says, "And we are definitely going to need sopapillas, so save room. They are amazing here."

My food never tasted so good. I savor the first bite, noticing all the onion, spices, and cheese. It is *heavenly*.

Chapter Twelve

THE SUMMER HAS passed by quickly. When we first got to Dad's, I was talking to Mom every day, but it has slowly tapered to once a week. She is mean and bitter and negative when she speaks. Sometimes slurring her words. Always miserable.

I feel guilty for not being there, but I also feel like I have come out of some sort of coma. Like I actually am able to make choices and take care of me and have fun. As long as Dad is willing to let me stay, this is where I want to be.

The new social worker has been out to see me a few times. We have talked about Mom and Dad, and even about Debbie. She asked me to see a counselor, and Dad set up one for me. Her name is Lesa and I really like her. She's helping me see some stuff I didn't see before. I am getting ready to go to school again too. The decision was made for us to continue to stay here beyond the summer. I'm super nervous about starting school, but I think it will be a fresh start for me. The school mascot here is a Demon. I have no idea what kind of mascot that is, and I think it's a bit ironic, given I ran from my demons.

I didn't really know how tired I was in my soul. Lesa said it is kinda like boiling a frog. If you put a frog in hot water, she will jump out right away because she knows it is hot. But, if you put the same frog in cool water and slowly raise the temperature, she will boil to death because she can't recognize the increasing heat. I know I am much smarter than a frog, but I can totally see that I almost boiled to death. I think my mom might be boiling to death herself.

Debbie is doing well. She found a job here at a food place. She has talked to Dad about maybe going to community college. She said she might be interested in pet grooming. It's cool to see Debbie think about the future. I also think it's funny to picture her holding upset dogs under running water for a living. It seems like just enough drama for her.

I hear my dad talking on the phone. It seems as though he's on with Mom, because of the short sentences he's getting in. He's had a lot of these calls lately.

He stops and listens, then responds, "Go ahead, Martha. I'm sure they'll see the sanity in taking Rachel away from her father and putting her back into a home with drugs and a woman who hasn't yet healed from the near-death she inflicted upon herself."

He slams down the phone and notices me looking at him. He looks slightly defeated until he sees me and his face lightens up.

"Dad, I'm sorry I caused so much trouble. Do you want me to go back to Mom's?"

"No." That is his short, powerful, loving answer. It's all he says as he grabs me and pulls me toward him in another of his signature bear hugs.

I love him.

✼ ✼ ✼

It is another hot, dry day in Golden, but it is horrifically humid in Cleveland in August when Mom commits her final, successful dramatic act.

Patty calls to let us know the police found her. Martha hadn't called in for her mandated therapy for three days.

I am numb.

I am sad.

I have no words.

I collapse onto the floor and cry.

✼ ✼ ✼

Today, I wrote a poem for Mom. We are going to the funeral tomorrow where I will read it. I miss her.

Stain

Mom, I remember the laughter, Eskimo kisses
Singing as loud as we could

Throwing dishes on the cement outside
So you could have chunks of ceramic to turn into art

Some made into beautiful mosaics
While others stayed in piles of disarray on the ground

Dangerous shards among the grass.

I remember the blood stain left on the carpet
Massaged out best I could

It wouldn't clean, wouldn't leave
It stays as a reminder

The stain you left on me was pain

Yet, like the mosaics you created,
Poured in was abounding love.

Love
The cement between the shards

Yes,
The stain you left on me was love

-Rachel White-Fraser

Leonard is at the funeral. He doesn't approach me until after it is over. I see him walking toward me. He looks messy, like he has hardly slept, and if he did, it was in his clothes. I'm not sure what to think, feel, or do.

I breathe.

He gives me a firm hug and holds it. His body feels weak and sad. He whispers into my ear, "I'm sorry."

Tears are in his eyes. He moves to Dad, not introducing himself to him, and shakes his hand. Debbie doesn't meet Leonard's eyes, so he briefly shakes her hand and moves towards the exit, alone. I feel for a moment an urge to reach out to him, like all those times he did that for me. Yet, he is so distant, so disconnected.

My dad's arm interlocks with mine and I watch Leonard leave. I picture holding him and kissing him the way I used to fantasize about him, but it feels weird now. Not because Mom is gone, but because of something else. I think I needed someone to listen to me. I needed someone who let me dream and go away from what I was feeling. I think I may have been that for Leonard, too, but I'm not sure. He's been through a lot lately and without talking to him, I just don't know. My therapist said I will understand even more as I continue to grieve and mature. I trust her.

I watch Debbie exit the reception and sit in a chair near Mom's grave. She is talking to Mom. I keep holding Dad's arm.

✳ ✳ ✳

Our old house smells the same and looks as it always has, but it has a new sense to it too. It is just memories now, no longer containing the vibrations of life. It feels stale and empty and alone. Kinda like how I feel.

Dad made arrangements to get rid of everything in the house that Debbie and I don't want, donating it all to the Salvation Army.

I take my personal stuff—my clothes, books, and blankets—most of which I've already replaced at Dad's, but want anyway. I also take the things that remind me of Mom. The things that tell stories about her that make me laugh and help me remember the good times. I take her favorite picture of me sticking out my tongue at her when I was little. I take her alarm clock. I take the James Patterson book she was reading, a corner folded down to mark her spot. The book she didn't finish like the life she didn't complete.

It's hard to believe it was merely months ago when I left this place so abruptly. So unexpectedly did my life change. It was only a short time ago when I met the man I'd only heard rumors about, my dad, and when I also opened my heart for Debbie and Tim. And here I am again, on this new abrupt, unexpected change. But I am more courageous this time. And I am okay.

It was hard and bumpy, but I kept going forward and things became okay again. I found my dad. And they will become okay again this time too. In this moment, when I feel so alone and scared, I also feel peace. Maybe for the first time ever.

With every confidence, I know I am loved uncon-ditionally. With complete certainty, I know my mom can't hurt herself anymore. I know, without fear, I will never again find my mother on the curb of conscious-ness, draped in blood or bone-white in clammy sweat.

And though my heart is broken, and life is unfair, and my world, THE world, will never be the same with-out her, she is at peace. Someday, I will be too—one day when the mark of her love is all that remains on my heart.

Epilogue

DEBBIE SITS IN a steel chair in the cemetery. Their father left a while ago to take Rachel to get her things. Meanwhile, she talks to the pile of dirt that holds her mother, as she never has before. Emotions she was never able to feel before come pouring out on the fresh grave. She tells her mother about the love and forgiveness and anger she held for her. And she offers her an apology.

She speaks until her father brushes her shoulder, bringing her back down to the ground she felt she had left some time ago. Feeling an amazing sense of relief, she blows a kiss to her mother. Not relief from the sadness, but a release of pent-up emotion. She feels as though forty years of tears have left her young body. She's never felt so high. And she is pleased. She will not be like her mother—for one, she has been drug-free for seventy-two days now and she knows she will never do that to herself again.

Debbie turns to her father and hugs him with every ounce of herself. "Dad, can I use your phone?"

"Now?" He asks, pulling his cell phone from its clip and handing it to her.

Debbie dials frantically, biting her lip and squinting her eyes as the phone rings on the other end.

"Hello," a voice answers.

"I love you, Tim. I do. I really, really love you." She smiles and then reaches for her father's hand.